ONLY AKIKO

BY
DUNCAN THORP

ONLY
AKIKO

Little, Brown and Company
BOSTON   TORONTO

Published simultaneously in Canada
by Little, Brown & Company (Canada) Limited

PRINTED IN THE UNITED STATES OF AMERICA

To Connie Gros

ONLY AKIKO

I

Late summer dawnlight overflowed the ruins of the port of Yokohama as the *AKA-53* groped tentatively up the roadstead. Bright buoys marked the channels freshly swept of mines and the brisk traffic of minesweepers and destroyers was a reminder that no one was taking chances. There were watchers on the ships and on the shore, moving slowly to an inevitable meeting and still helpless to fix on an attitude that would cover the strangeness of their coming face to face.

Hank leaned on the ship's rail, looking at Japan — his first close look. The great port city looked dead — or dying, anyway — a jumble of blackened rubble, desolate and crumbling piers. A few sunken hulks were indicated by slanted and tattered mastheads emerging from the bay. He saw the twisted girders of half-finished vessels in a pair of launchways on his extreme left. Behind the waterfront, stretching away to his right, lay the blackened stumps and roots of a great wasted city. This was the heavy-industry section between Yokohama and Tokyo that the earnest young lecturer had emphasized so thoroughly in the indoctrination class on Okinawa. Now with the light growing stronger you could begin to tell the ruins of the big buildings from those of the ordinary dwellings, the larger, more rugged heaps of rubble, made of concrete and brick, contrasting with the little rectangles where only pottery shards and ashes remained of the original houses.

"It's like an insect," he thought, "a crippled and almost dead insect, black and smashed and lying on its back." Two great dockside cranes were moving at different points on the waterfront, waving their clawed and skeletal arms over their cargo holds, and they were like the insect's legs — his last two good ones still trying gamely to do the job they were made to do.

Behind the bomb-broken and flame-twisted waterfront wreckage the mountains were growing blue and serene. Fuji's perfect cone, snow-tipped and instantly recognizable, he was just able to see, and as he watched, the snowcap turned delicately pink in the morning light. He looked around now at the soldiers and sailors moving on the deck with the red light coloring their faces. Neat high lights flamed on the polished combat helmets and lightly colored the chalk numbers of the helmet fronts which would identify each man during the debarkation.

A few minutes earlier Warrant Officer Zobel had dismissed the muster of the 91st Army Engineers Battalion who were to establish the GHQ motor pool in Tokyo. Most of the men had scattered swiftly to their compartments, mysteriously intent upon last-minute preparations for the landing. Below decks Hank knew there would be surreptitious stowage of accumulated stocks of cigarettes, toilet soap, and chewing gum by the foresighted soldiers. Experience or rumor had convinced many soldiers that these goods would bring them treasures in exchange

Some of the men were admittedly apprehensive and many were secretly expecting trouble. A few of them were secreting personal weapons — short-barreled souvenir pistols that could be strapped below the knee under the trouser leg or slender switch-blade knives that were even easier to hide. Every man had his M-1 rifle, of course, but it was off duty where trouble started.

Three men from the outfit had remained on deck and they had moved to the rail to join Hank. They were silent, intent on the approach to the dock, searching as though for a clue in the wastes of the waterfront.

"All the ships and men," Hank thought, "took a long time getting used to war, and now just when they really know what to do about it, they have to get used to peace. It's almost what they call an embarrassing situation."

Wheeler, the young Pfc, broke in, moving closer on the rail to the big sergeant.

"You buyin' that stuff in the Old Man's Emily Post book, Hank?" Wheeler went on quickly without waiting for an answer. "Of course I'm going to follow orders, but I don't intend to take anything offa *them*. You know what they'd be doing to us if it was them landing in San Francisco, ain't that right?"

[5]

"Just play it by ear, Wheeler," said the sergeant soothingly. "Maybe they're worried about us."

"Well," said the private dubiously, "that's all right, I guess. But I'm gonna keep my eyes peeled every minute. You can't trust a Jap and they all look alike, and you can't tell what they're thinking."

The warrant officer, Johnny Zobel, nursing his everlasting hangover, eyed Wheeler sourly.

"Whatya know about Japs? You ain't ever seen one outside a movie. From what I've seen they all belong dead. This MacArthur honeymoon gonna last till they find the first dozen AWOL's floating down the river. Me, I'm still on a wartime basis except when the Jap lovers is looking." Zobel nodded and smiled grimly to himself.

"Maybe it's like Hank says," said the stout sergeant with the graying temples and the four hash marks. "Maybe they're scared all to hell of us and dyin' to cooperate. What you aim to do, Hank, if this here Japan turns out to be a land of golden opportunity?"

"Just move in easy," the big sergeant said. "I'm reserving judgment until I find out."

He turned away from the white-tipped mountain and the stricken city, hooked elbows on the rail, and faced inboard. He doffed his helmet, wiped the sweatband carefully with a handkerchief, and left it dangling negligently by the chin strap.

The small breeze buffed his close-cropped wheat-straw hair. He wore the often seen face of millions of combat-matured young men, stripped of its overburden of vanity and innocence to the bedrock of quick manhood — responsible, intelligent, proud. The other men, even Wheeler, listened more carefully when he spoke than they did to each other.

"I'm holding out on Len," he thought. "I'm a little over-trained after four years, myself, which is why I'm here. I was a three weeks' civilian, as proud of that discharge chit as anyone. Three weeks — and one happy little family dinner and I was back at the recruiting desk crying to be taken in.

"If it hadn't been for Cousin Raymond and Cousin Lester I might have gone on to college. Aunt Mary didn't help either, bless her blundering, well-meaning tongue. 'Tell them, Henry,' she says, 'about getting wounded and all those terrible times you had in the Pacific. Raymond and Lester were so fortunate getting deferred, I've always thought.'

" 'Oh, do tell us,' says Cousin Raymond. 'Tell us all over again what we read in the papers, and had read to us so many lovely times in your letters home, and have heard any God's number of times from all the relatives — how you upheld the honor of the Muellers while Lester and I dodged the draft.' And then it was Lester making everything cozy. 'So we didn't get a Purple Heart. So we bought a ranch, and it made money, to our everlasting shame. But let me tell you, Henry — wait five years and not one soul will remember that you were wounded or whether you were even in the war. They'll just remember us, because we have a little money and that's what people don't forget.' "

He flipped the helmet in a swift circle on his wrist and let it rock slowly to rest. The other three were leaning on the rail, calling each other's attention to objects and people on the docks as the ship swung slowly and headed toward a slip. He resolutely capped his seething memory of the hateful Sunday dinner and the other times the vicious defensiveness of the cousins and their wives had welled over like a poisonous pool. He swung again and looked over the rail, and spoke to the older sergeant.

"I wonder how those two cranes managed to come through the bombing. We're the first troops in here, and they must have been in working order. Everything else is knocked flat."

"You know how it goes, Hank," said Len Whitely. "We work over a rock with the heavy stuff, and then comes the Navy and shells it three days nonstop. Every tree and bush is made into toothpicks and the stones into powder. What do we find when we move in — waitin' for us on the beach? Four pigs and a goat without a scratch. We ain't quite perfect yet."

They fell silent as the ship groped toward the projecting piers in a slow turn. "I got to quit expecting things," Hank thought. "There's nothing to get excited about, just another ship landing on a bomb-battered beach, and we've seen plenty of that. No matter what you imagine you'll find, it's always different — usually a disappointment."

He fell into an old habit of addressing himself directly and silently. "But we still get excited like a kid going to a ball game, don't we, Hank, old son? You'll never be able to quit, and you know it. Every time your journey ends you hold your breath — maybe this time you'll find love and gold and adventure — maybe this is the place you're looking for. So have at it, my romantic old buddy, it won't be for always. If you look in too many places, too many times, for too many years, I expect you'll get over it."

"Here comes the mayor's welcoming committee," said Len, nodding toward the pier. A group of American sailors trotted smartly down the pier. Men broke off and stood by the bollards at intervals where the ship's lines were intended to be secured. A little behind them came a group of small brown-faced men in baggy ragged trousers, shirtless and with white rags wound about their foreheads. They arranged themselves deferentially behind the waiting sailors. The ship slid close to the dockside, shuddered abruptly in reverse, and lay still. Heaving lines with their weighted monkey fists were whipped expertly toward the pier by the ship's crew. The sailors waiting on the pier grabbed the heaving lines and began towing the heavy cables toward the bollard.

Three of the sailors missed their heaving lines because they were watching their Japanese counterparts too closely. Instantly the Japanese men snatched up the heaving lines. The sailors bristled visibly and moved menacingly toward the three civilians. With flashing smiles and polite bows the Japanese longshoremen handed the lines to the sailors. The sailors took the lines and smiled back. When the heavy mooring lines reached the pier, the Japanese workers helped haul the cable eyes to the bollards, a sailor and a native to each line. When the ship's lines were fast and the straining winches began lugging the ship sideway against the pier, the Japanese men bowed politely again and moved away.

The men watching on the ship missed none of this. Hank looked quickly at Len.

"I think it's gonna be all right," he said. The men turned away, immediately intent on their well-rehearsed formula for the debarkation. The sun was higher and the mountains were partly screened in blue haze.

2

_____

ON THE twenty-ninth day after the armistice, in the Shinjuku district of Tokyo, two Japanese girls knelt on the frayed *tatami* matting that floored the narrow gallery of their tiny apartment. The paper and wood panels fronting the street were drawn back to funnel in the attenuated October sunshine. One girl was small and doll-like. Her kimono and obi were of fashionable material and her freshly oiled hair gleamed wet and black on her shoulders. They had just returned from the public bath in the next block and were reveling briefly in the midmorning sun before putting up their hair. Her companion was a taller girl with heavier lips and slower movements. Their talk was of the one breath-catching subject that occupied everyone in Shinjuku, and, indeed, everyone in the Chrysanthemum Empire.

"I heard today," said Kiyoko, "there are thousands of them around Yuraku Station. The great American General MacArsar-san and many of their high officers and noblemen do business now in the Daiichi Building. They have taken the Imperial Hotel and also the Yuraku Hotel to live in. All the people in the offices were killed to make room for them. They pay the young girls very good money to work for them, but they rape and abuse them, and they are so fierce the girls die every week and have to be replaced."

Little Akiko was considerably less of an alarmist than her companion. "I believe only what I see," she said. "I hear of rapes and killing, but it is always a story the speaker has heard on the wind. My friend Chang showed me a book — a little book that the Americans give to the soldiers to teach them how to ask for things politely. They are to pay money for what they wish to buy from the shops, and in the book it says they are ordered by their officers not to touch the women of Japan. Chang is a Chinese and consequently more intelligent than Japanese people. He lived for seven years in the United States in the city of Chicago, and he can read their writing."

"But they have blue eyes," said Kiyoko. "The old woman who sells *sushi* in Hamabaku says the ones with the blue eyes are the most evil. If one looks them squarely in the eyes, she is in their power and possessed of devils. Afterwards she must do what the foreigners say, and she walks like a ghost without knowing what she is doing."

"Foolish cousin," said Akiko. "This is the superstitious nonsense they teach you in the country. You are always saying such things, but you do not believe them, do you? Or else you would have gone back to Omiya before the foreigners came. You do not wish to escape their attentions, perhaps."

"How about you?" Kiyoko was nettled. "You are thinking, as always, of one thing: will they have much money and be generous."

"That is so, so, so," Akiko admitted, the long black eyes in the little toy face slitted against the sunlight. "We must think of money always. It is no use any more to go to teahouses where the students used to drink. They are all closed. The only men left are few enough and all too young — no money. In another week the last of the old rice will be gone and now we must begin to eat fish with the night meal only every other day."

Akiko stood up and shook the loose cloud of freshly washed hair over her shoulders.

"Hurry, Miss Lazy-legs. We must finish our hair and wash some clothes and then make a plan. I wish you would make the plans sometimes. I have to make them all — and then you grumble if it does not turn out well."

Getting no answer, Akiko turned again to her cousin and saw Kiyoko transfixed, staring up the street, her mouth an O of amazement. Akiko shielded her eyes under her palm and looked into the brilliant sunlight toward the approaching jeep.

"Quick," chattered Kiyoko. "Into the room and slide the doors. If they see us, it will be all up with us."

"No, be quiet." Akiko stood straight and took her hand from her eyes languidly as the jeep approached and the angle of the sunlight changed.

"Oh, oh," moaned Kiyoko in an agony of apprehension, still cross-legged on the *tatami* matting and half crouched in the shadow of Akiko's kimono.

The jeep cruised in low gear through the rubble and litter of the narrow street. There were two men in the rear seat and a driver. The pair in the rear were older. They spoke earnestly to each other, and one of them was smoking a cigarette. The driver was a young man who concentrated on his driving and did not speak to the other two. He sat alone in the front seat, occasionally whipping a quick appraising glance along the house fronts at the street edge.

Certainly he had the whitest of skins, the bluest of eyes, and the cowlick of hair underneath his overseas cap was as yellow as the sunshine on a new *tatami* mat. Akiko stared with unmannerly intensity until the blue eyes flicked in her direction. The driver's gaze moved easily over her still figure and came to rest on her face. The white face split in a swift smile, one blue eye closed in a confidential wink, and the driver resumed his regard of the street with a sincerity far beyond the call of duty.

Akiko stood for perhaps three seconds while she felt his eyes upon her. Then she allowed his glance to meet her eyes, dropped them modestly when he smiled, but just as the jeep passed she let a little ghost of a smile scamper across her lips. She remained motionless with downcast eyes.

It was perfect timing. The sergeant was *almost* sure she had smiled at him.

Kiyoko crouched, head bent to her knees, until the Americans and the jeep were safely past.

"Get up," said Akiko, laughing. "I have looked into the blue eyes, and I am as well as ever. I think I am going to get along with these people."

Kiyoko stood up but turned about aimlessly while Akiko cleared the bowls from the cluttered breakfast table. She was easily distracted, and the close encounter with the passing Americans had rendered her more witless than usual.

"What shall we do today, Cousin?" she asked humbly. Kiyoko was completely awed by Akiko's demonstration of courage.

Akiko smiled. "Now I have a plan," she said. "I will go to Chang's and ask him to teach me English speaking. He has lusted for me for weeks since his mistress Mioshi left. It is lucky for us that no money will be required. You may come and listen and perhaps you may pick up a few words. Come, tall cousin, we will share his knowledge of languages and perhaps his new rice."

On the fourth day after the jeep had passed there was a hesitant tapping at the sliding door of the girls' apartment.

"What is it?" said Akiko.

"*Kombanwa*," said a voice — a young man's voice with a peculiar accent.

Akiko unlocked the sliding door and rolled it back slowly. Before her stood the blond jeep driver, his arms full of packages. He snatched off his overseas cap but dropped several packages in the process.

"*Kombanwa,*" he repeated doggedly. It was the Japanese word for "Good evening," patiently coached into him by a nisei interpreter. It was reputed to open the door to a Japanese house but was not guaranteed to keep it open. Fearful that she might close the door before his good intentions were manifest, the tall American boy retrieved his packages hastily. He moved a step nearer and repeated his Sesame for the third time.

"*Kombanwa.*"

"*Kombanwa,*" Akiko replied politely and stood aside. Then for good measure she added an English greeting.

"Hey-yo."

Seeing his confusion, she knelt at the edge of the gallery and patted the *tatami* floor, indicating that he was to sit beside her. The soldier sat down, still clutching his packages. Akiko knelt swiftly at his feet, untied his shoes, and removed them. The shoes looked tremendous in her tiny brown hands. She placed the well-polished shoes carefully, toes down, in an umbrella stand, and then she showed him how to swing around and stand on the gallery without soiling his socks on the muddy floor of the street-level entrance. She slid back an inner door, and they entered her room, although the American had to duck to clear the doorway.

Kiyoko looked, gasped, covered her face with her hands, and burst into a fit of hysterical giggles. Akiko looked at her contemptuously.

"She name Kiyoko."

"*Kombanwa*," said the soldier desperately to the giggling Kiyoko. The result was wilder giggles and an attempt to hide her face that looked as though she wanted to push her head between her legs.

"I name Akiko." She pointed elaborately at her bosom.

"I name Hank Mueller," said the soldier, tapping his chest in turn. He was much relieved to say something besides "*Kombanwa.*"

Akiko addressed herself to her roommate in crackling Japanese. Her rapid flow of language sounded like the clatter of small bells, but the tone to Hank was of one who gives orders and expects results. Kiyoko's giggles subsided promptly. She rose and backed from the room, making a deep obeisance to the soldier as she withdrew.

Akiko took a small table which stood on edge against the wall of the little room and placed it in the middle of the floor. It stood just about a foot above the woven straw matting which made up the floor. She took a pile of cushions from a corner, placed most of them at one side of the table, and motioned Hank to sit on them. He squatted down on them tailor fashion. Akiko knelt across the table from him and smiled brightly.

"You speak English?" the soldier asked.

"No speak," said Akiko sadly, then added in Japanese, "Pardon me, I am only a stupid girl."

"I name Hank Mueller," he said again, pointing to himself.

"Ank Mirror," said Akiko hesitantly, and then she

[17]

smiled again, seeing the American boy looked pleased. Her confidence was growing rapidly. Why, this was only a boy, younger than herself by at least four years, she judged. But what a giant in size!

"You Akiko," said the soldier, pointing to her across the table. He pronounced her name correctly, Ah-kee-ko, putting the stress on the first syllable as she had done.

"Watanabe Akiko," the Japanese girl amplified, while smiling vigorously to encourage his pronunciation.

"American speak," said Henry, "Akiko Watanabe."

"So, so," shouted Akiko gleefully in jubilant agreement. Here finally was a matter she understood. Chang had informed her that the foreigners always reversed Japanese names, using the family name last. Here was education coming home to roost.

But now the conversation languished. The soldier looked about the room, eyed the scroll in the alcove, the vase of dried flowers beneath, the little dressing table in the corner where the girls performed their toilets. He took reassurance from such familiar objects as a box of face powder, a fragment of lipstick, and a snapshot of Akiko in a cheap frame. This showed her in a neat schoolgirl's middy suit with braids down her shoulders.

"You schoolgirl," declared the soldier, pointing to the picture, but Akiko shook her head miserably. Then she brightened and took the picture.

"Akiko," she said, pointing first to the picture and then to herself. She made a sweeping gesture, plainly indicating a period of time, and then said, "Before."

This was good for mutual smiles and vigorous head nodding on both sides of the table. They were both learning. Now the screen on one side of the room slid back, and Kiyoko bowed her head to the matting. Then rising and picking up a tray beside her, she started setting the table.

First was a clay vessel glowing with charcoal embers over which she placed a small brass teakettle. Bowls were set for three and a pair of chopsticks laid beside each bowl. Akiko put tea in the kettle, and when it had steeped, poured it into the bowls. Each of the three took tea and regarded one another owlishly. Hank had trouble holding the bowl because it had no handles. Akiko, bolder by this time, placed his hands so that the bowl rested flat on the palm of his left and his right hand tilted the bowl to drink.

Kiyoko produced strange dishes of food and used the rest of the hot water in a saucepan. This she placed again on the cooking pot and poured into it a quantity of rice. Hank inspected the food with some suspicion and then suddenly recalled his packages. He reached behind him and recovered the cartons scattered on the *tatami* floor. Quickly he opened a box of Hershey bars.

"Chocolate," he announced, presenting them to Akiko. He opened another box and gave it to Kiyoko. Both girls recognized the chocolate immediately, for it was ever so rare and much desired.

"*Domo arigato gozaimasu,*" said both girls together, making a deep bow at the same time. It was obvious they were saying "Thank you."

[19   ]

Hank produced a salt box full of sugar. "Sugar," he stated, presenting it to Akiko. Again understanding was immediate and complete. *Sugar* was one of the first three words which Akiko had required of her teacher, Chang. The girls teamed up again to bow and repeat their litany of thanks.

"*Domo arigato gozaimasu.*"

"Cigarettes," Hank declaimed, presenting each girl with a pack of Luckies.

"*Domo arigato gozaimasu.*"

The bundles were now empty. Hank offered cigarettes from his own pack and all three smoked happily. Hank lighted Akiko's cigarette with his lighter while Kiyoko took a pair of iron chopsticks, plucked an ember from the cooking pot, and lighted her own. Immediately Akiko took Hank's lighter and indicated it was to be left on the table with his cigarettes.

For a time the girls chattered in Japanese. Then Kiyoko served the rice in the same tea bowls. Hank was helpless with the chopsticks, so Akiko deftly formed the rice into bite-sized balls and popped them into his mouth. Between bites she offered him bits of the other dishes. He recognized a grayish-green mass as some sort of pickled cabbage and suffered a swallow or two. He ate a few morsels of pulpy white meat which he thought to be seafood of some sort. The bits were first immersed by Akiko in a sharp sauce of spiced oil and mustard. It was peppery and pleasant.

Presently he picked up one of his chopsticks and speared

one of the little gobs of white flesh. About to swab it in the sauce he paused and lifted the morsel to his nose. A sniff confirmed his suspicions.

"Jesus," he said, "raw fish and I haven't been here an hour."

Hank managed to pantomime his desire for a little hot water in the pan. Then he tried to ask for salt. A vigorous shaking of a hypothetical saltceller merely mystified the girls. Finally Akiko understood he wanted something in the line of food and snapped an order at her companion. Kiyoko was off like a shot, returning immediately with two badly dehydrated sweet potatoes. Hank shook his head. Akiko whipped out another command and Kiyoko made another round trip to the kitchen. One by one they produced every item of their larder. When they got down to several kinds of spice, they could see by his face they were getting warm. At last the salt was produced.

Hank added salt to the boiling water in the pan and popped in several pieces of the fish. The girls regarded the process as though they feared an explosion. They relaxed, while the fish boiled, over more tea and cigarettes. Akiko now lit Hank's cigarette with his lighter, then laid it on the table and lit her own with a coal fished from the *hibachi*. So did Kiyoko. In a moment Hank sampled the fish. He ate three little morsels with gusto and offered bits to the girls. They sampled it with apprehension but found it palatable and ate a little, with squeals of appreciation and a great deal of laughter. The meal was finally finished, topped off with Hershey bars and more tea. The dishes were borne away by Kiyoko, and the silence came down again. Kiyoko did not return.

Timidly Akiko moved to Hank's side and knelt while she examined his left sleeve with great care. Running her fingers over the chevrons, she inquired, "You capating?"

"No captain," said Henry. "Sergeant." He patted the sleeve. "Sergeant Hank."

"Sharzen Ank," said Akiko painstakingly, her eyes on his face. They said no more.

"Kee-rist," thought Henry. "I thought they were all slant-eyed. This little old bug has eyes that are almost round when she opens them up. They just get slanty when she laughs. I can see this one's got the class. I'll bet the other one's her maid or her kid sister and has to wait on her.

"Now what the hell do I do? If I put my hand on her leg and she yells bloody murder, I've had it. They say these Japs don't kiss their women, so if I kiss her, maybe she'll get scared. Oh, balls, I gotta get back to the barracks by twenty-three hundred, and I haven't got all night. Here goes—"

He slid his left arm tentatively around her and put the fingers of his right hand gently on the delicate golden cheek to tilt her face. She moved easily, like fluid, in his arms. The little doll face tilted up to his and the jet eyes stared trustingly into the blue eyes. They kissed.

Lightly, easily at first, then harder, then avidly with parting lips — and all the while with open eyes reading each other's face. Then the baby-sweet expression vanished

[22]

suddenly from her eyes and they glazed to a flat reptilian glitter. Her breath came shudderingly from her tiny body, and her movements now, in his arms, were old and familiar as all of life.

Stupid with passion he tore with frantic fingers to free himself of his clothing. The light went out suddenly, a key rattled as the sliding doors were locked, a bedroll appeared in an instant from behind another sliding screen, and she was back in his arms, wearing only a coarse shift, helping his fumbling fingers, petal lips drinking insatiably from his mouth, all urgency and strange grace, and silken skin beyond believing.

And the superincumbent moment came down on them. Behind his closed lids all was a red-lit wilderness that hummed and sang. Delight bloomed lamplike within him and spread like slow light waves from the core of being to the delicate nerve fronds, ending on the skin's surface, relieving tension, softening the tautened limbs, and dying at last in a languorous sunset of ecstasy.

Buck Sergeant Henry Mueller, U. S. Army Engineers, 91st Battalion, late of Los Angeles, twenty-four years of age, graduate of a sexual encounter with a middle-aged female lush at seventeen, postgraduate of two brief classes in a Mexicali brothel at nineteen, had found him a woman. Even in his disappointments he had never lost faith. Somewhere on this planet was a woman for him, and it would be just like this.

3

Winter rain splashed the roof tiles over their heads as Akiko faced her stepmother across the steaming kettle and the tea bowls. Kiyoko had obligingly made herself scarce after serving tea. Now they were alone, anticipating the rare opportunity for womanly confidences even as they dreaded the risk of embarrassment. The visits of Mother Watanabe, once or twice a year, were occasions of great delicacy.

Mama-san came directly to the point with a flick of her eyes at the khaki uniform hanging on a wire hanger on the bedroom-door screen.

"You have friends among the foreigners?"

Akiko was distressed at her mother's use of the plural. She wished to be credited for departing from habitual promiscuity, however temporary the situation, and however circumstantial the reasons.

"I have *one* friend," she corrected humbly, "an American *gunso* — or Sergeant, as they say — who expresses a small admiration. He is the only one."

"All is changed with the coming of these foreigners," sighed Mama-san. "Even now the family is restless. Your sister Yōko wishes to study their language and to apply for a position in an officers' place of entertainment. Your father opposes."

"As usual." Akiko could not keep the sneer from her voice. "He fears he will not be able to collect her income."

"Always the hatred, First Child. Remember, he is your father. Now, no — do not protest. I cannot listen and I know your feeling. It is perhaps not easy to respect him. But if only he had felt about you as I did when first I saw you, we would have been happy, perhaps, and many things would be different today."

"Tell me again," Akiko begged ardently, "how it was when he brought me to you. I love to hear you tell it."

Mama-san took tea and stared into the amber bowl. She told the story for the hundredth and more time.

"Well, then, it was all those years and years ago. We were just married and very happy and I did not know of your existence at all. One day (it was in the time of plum blossoms, I remember) he brought you to the house, all in a fine kimono, and he said, 'Here is my daughter. If you will keep her, she may stay. If you will not have her, I will sell her.'

"Oh, you can imagine what pain I felt. For a moment I could not think. I turned my face away and I was about to say, 'Take her away,' but I heard the little rustle of your dress as you made your obeisance so I looked just a trifle from the corner of my eye.

[25]

"You bowed sweetly and with grace, not with the up-thrust rump of a country girl, and you were so sweet and dainty I remembered Prince Genji and his lovely ward. It was somewhat like a legend of the old times, but I hardened my heart and I made to speak across your bowed head: 'Take her away.'

"But just then you peeked above your hands to steal a look at my face. And when I saw your baby face, so sweet and curious and so naughty, I held my tongue. And though you quickly dropped your eyes as I observed them, they went straight into my heart, and love flowed into my heart like a wave into a cave by the sea. And so you were born to me as all children are born in a little time of much pain and much love."

Akiko knelt, enraptured, on her cushion. She never tired of this old story. Her love for her foster mother was the only true thing in all her life. When she heard the story, it brought a redeeming bath of high emotion that washed away the acid bite of bitterness and waste. It brought quick tears and she shook her head, embarrassed, and tried to speak.

Mama-san put down her tea bowl firmly. There was a long and embarrassing silence, while the rain sizzled on the tiles and the kettle steamed slowly on the *hibachi*.

"If I had only kept her close to me," thought the mother. "But after that business with that dog of a student I thought it best to send her into business. And now, what has she become? I really know very little — she has these properties, but no regular employment. She is dutiful and generous, but where does she get the money? And all the clothes? It is better, perhaps, not to inquire too closely. It is too late and I can do nothing more.

"But it is not her mother's blood that makes her so headstrong and willful, as I once imagined. It is from her father, for already I see the same signs in Yōko. But Yōko will not quarrel with the father; only by her own sly means she will persist in having her own way; and she will depend on her sweet face and beautiful figure to dispel my doubts — as she has always done. Akiko is really more honest."

Akiko had been restlessly moving the tea things about. Her mother's silence seemed an accusation, and she felt compelled to explain.

"The Americans are not as we were told," she said rapidly. "There is something of kindness and courtesy in them — not just the loud voices and brazen manners we sometimes observe — as for that, I could tell you about the manners of Japanese officers in Manchukuo that would—"

Mama-san interrupted her with a gesture. "Hush, child — I cannot listen to your lies and I must not listen to the truth. I have taken your money and we have eaten the rice that it has bought. And now we take tea and weep together once or twice a year. But *foreigners* —"

"He is gentle and kind," said Akiko. "And generous. A little happiness gives him much delight. He is not like other men."

"Then you are in love," said Mama-san positively.

"What a thing to say! Pardon me, Little Mother, but Akiko in love! Never. You know I want no husband nor many children — poverty, hard work, and a blow in the face when the man comes home drunk. I am no Lady of the Shadows to wait all the years for some brute of a man to notice my devotion. No, I have my own way — and not so bad at that. There is the rent from the two houses and the fine American gifts from the sergeant. He brings me sugar, chocolate, cigarettes — all things that can be turned to account — and there will be more.

"I shall grow old and mean — and wealthy. Someday there will be many houses, and a hundred families will bring me rents."

"All the same," said Mama-san quietly, "I observe changes. But tell me of these foreigners. Now and then I see them in the streets. Not all of them have blue eyes. Do you think it is true they have enormous houses and great wealth in their country?"

"I think it is true," said Akiko thoughtfully. "At first I thought my friend was boasting. Later I came to realize few of these Americans have any skill in lying. They tell the truth because they can afford to, although it sounds somewhat offensive to our ears. Well, my friend says they have all those automobiles, of course, and the humblest of them can go to the cinema every night. Their women wear expensive clothes and earn their own money. He comes from California, which is on the sea, and the weather is warmer than on Kyushu. Women choose their husbands freely by mingling together at marriageable age. And these men treat them with great respect and take great pride in the woman's happiness. And when I do not understand him or do a stupid thing, my friend only laughs as one does at a small child."

"He will go away, Akiko-san. Someday they will all go back to the United States."

"Yes," Akiko said. "Someday he will go—"

Mama-san rose from the cushion and arranged the fold of her kimono. "All the same," she said, looking again at the uniform on the wire hanger, "I perceive that it is beginning. You have learned many things I shall never know, but the love of a man — you know nothing — nothing at all."

Akiko knelt down at the street entrance and placed the clogs on her mother's feet. Standing up, she thrust a roll of bills quickly inside Mama-san's kimono sleeve.

"For Yōko's language lessons," she said. "No, no, Mama-san, it is all right. It is from the rent money. Quickly now, while I hold your parasol — the rickshaw is waiting."

4

A PROPERLY brought-up Japanese girl is a model of politeness, self-effacement, and virtue. Akiko broke the mold. Not as a result of wartime relaxation of family control, not as a result of the example of the bold Western women who flocked to Tokyo later in the occupation, nor yet from the corruption of free-spending servicemen. She did it all by herself long before the Americans got there.

Akiko supposed herself to be the illegitimate daughter of a talented geisha, the result of one of her father's youthful indiscretions. After she was established in her stepmother's home, her half brothers and sisters came in regular succession. First her brother Taiji, and then her beautiful sister Yōko. Then Papa Watanabe fathered Sumiko from an extramarital alliance with a country girl. She was incorporated into the family as a matter of course. Finally came little Kimiko, a sparkling jewel of a child, to celebrate the mother's retirement from a decade of wildly unplanned parenthood.

Somehow the mother supported the family through the more desperate stretches, since she had a steady income as a dressmaker. In fact, Mother Watanabe had an enviable reputation as the best maker of ceremonial kimonos in Shinjuku and Nakano.

Papa-san, who had a better than average education, became a sharp-witted chiseler around the teahouses of the Tokyo financial district. Occasionally he got a piece of "a good thing." These fortunes were rare, since it took a highly specific type of enterprise to fit Papa-san's talents. He specialized in operations wherein the investment was nil, the legality doubtful, the risks monumental, and the rewards occasionally handsome.

At times there were, then, these brief periods of affluence. Family diet improved. There were fine kimonos and dancing lessons for the girls and plans for Taiji's career as a naval cadet at Yokosuka. But these lasted just so long as it took the geishas, whores, and sake houses to swallow the bankroll. Then the family settled back to the lean months on Mama-san's steady pittance as a dressmaker.

After Akiko's defloration in University Park by a young student (who prudently dropped out of sight) and the consequent turmoil in the Watanabe family, Mama-san installed the plan for Akiko's business career with every indication of ultimate success. Eldest Daughter became a model of deportment. She avoided her father as much as possible, but spoke politely of him, whether he was drunk or sober, on such occasions as required speech. Only Mother Watanabe knew anything of the depth of Akiko's hatred, and even her indulgent heart would have shriveled if she had known it all.

Akiko quickly forgot the hasty affair in the park. It had been exciting at first, then painful. She never forgot the blows of her father and the blood in her mouth. She learned how to wait. Her only mistake, she felt, had been in attempting something beyond her experience. Yet, she knew, somewhere in this mysterious drive that made a man helpless for want of a woman was a species of power. It was a great power that required study and apprentice-ship — she must learn the secrets by which the power could be controlled. So for a time she waited.

Akiko was exceptionally well dressed (in consequence of one of Papa-san's little deals) on a day in 1939 when she applied for the position of clerk with the New Man-churian Coal Company. Papa-san accompanied her to the old Kaijo Building, introduced her to the acquaintance who had promised to speak for her, and left for a teahouse with a purse burning a hole in his sleeve.

After filling out various forms and demonstrating to an older secretary her facility with commercial ideographs, the abacus, and a typewriter, she was presented to one of the junior executives together with the examples of her work.

Fujita Hisao at this time was thirty-eight years old and a rising young man in the New Manchurian Coal Company. He was henpecked and timid, having married an older and wealthier woman, daughter of a major stockholder,

but he had an eye for little fresh-faced girls from the sub-
urbs, most especially small ones dressed in exquisitely sewn
kimonos who walked with just a suggestion of the erotic
mince of the geishas.

Akiko did well with the New Manchurian Coal Company, almost suspiciously well. In a few months her wardrobe threatened to crowd the little Watanabe house in
Shinjuku. When Papa-san questioned her sharply, she fore-
saw that matters could not continue so profitably while
she was under his avaricious eye, so she moved into private
lodging.

After long urging by Mama-san, Watanabe paid a visit
of polite inquiry to the offices in the old Kaijo Building.
In the most poetic terms he was told to mind his own
business and sent away.

After that, Akiko began dropping in for a family visit on
weekends or holidays, usually arriving just after Papa-san
had left the house. She worshiped her mother and felt
proud when she was able to bring presents for her brothers and sisters. She never came without bringing clothing
or food, and always on leaving, slipped a bundle of yen
notes in her mother's rough hand. Mama-san accepted
the money with tears.

Social triangles in Japan, wherein one corner lies in the
home office, follow an international pattern. Little whispers
grew to wholesale rumor. Money was quietly spent to establish certain indelicate evidence. Handsome Hisao, he with
the air of a samurai and the soul of a rabbit, found his
delightful secretary an embarrassment to his career.

He called for her when she came to the office one morning and Akiko entered with the exaggerated mincing walk that always excited him. Only for him she wore the bashful smile and liquid sidelong glance that paid so well. But there was not the customary response in his boyish face this day — only exasperation, weakness, and worry.

"Well, then, little one," he began abruptly, "how would you like a new position? An advance in your salary, of course, but all in all a lucky thing for you — after such a brief experience with our company."

"I am unworthy," Akiko demurred politely. "I am only a stupid girl already deep in your debt for many kindnesses. But if it pleases you —"

"I am a man of many affairs — heavy responsibilities. My wife (she is the president's daughter, I think you know) has great concern, since she has heard certain rumors. In short, I am required to make arrangements which do not please me and which will cause you much heaviness of heart. This new position I speak of is far away. We will not see each other —"

"But that is unbelievable!" cried Akiko. "What position, however well paid, could measure the loss of your company? Do not speak of this, I beg of you."

"I must," he said angrily. "Be quiet, girl. There is a fine position for a secretary-bookkeeper at the company mine office not far from Harbin. You will have three times your present salary and your travel all paid on a fine ship."

"It will be dirty and cold." Akiko began to cry. "I will

be crowded with steerage passengers and I can't stand the filth and bad food."

"You will travel first class, of course," Hisao assured her hastily. "I will arrange with the captain for the best accommodations. Now, do not cry, Akiko-san."

"Who will protect me?" wailed Akiko. "It is a savage country full of bandits and beasts. Nothing but rough miners — I couldn't stand it."

"Foolishness. Manchuria is orderly under our Army. Our mines have managers, executives, engineers. There are a few families and one or two women. I really thought you would be more sensible."

"I have no proper clothes for the cold climate," sniffed Akiko. "No doubt I will freeze the first winter."

"Our offices are coal-heated, of course. As for clothes — that will be arranged. And I had thought I might buy you a farewell gift, something appropriate to a sad occasion — sad for both of us, you know."

"If I could only stay in Tokyo," she pleaded. "Even if we never saw each other. If I could but wait in the street to see you enter and leave your house, I could bear it better."

"No, no!" he shouted. "That is exactly what you must *not* do. You do not understand the workings of large-scale financing — an indiscretion can ruin a businessman."

Akiko straightened her slumped shoulders with pitiful dignity. "It is too heavy a load for an ignorant girl to bear. It would be better if I killed myself one night in that little room we shared." She shook her head and two little tears flipped right and left from her dimpled cheeks.

[35]

"Never!" he cried, with hysteria rising in his voice. He jumped from his chair and stood over her. "Little one, listen to me. A suicide would ruin me utterly. You *must* go to Manchuria for my sake. The salary will be *four times* what we pay you here. You shall have a whole houseful of new clothes."

"And a present, you said," said Akiko, very woebegone. "You will give me a small jewel to take the place of my heart."

"As *big* as your heart," he vowed ardently. "You will see the price of my sacrifice — only do not speak of suicide and waiting in the street. Go now and start buying the pretty things for your trip — here is money for a start."

"Since you desire it, I will try," she said. "But my heart is dead from this moment." The small hand closed gently around the roll of money.

Outside, in the street, she counted the money carefully and replaced it in her kimono sleeve. For a second she stared reflectively at the sky, then her thin shoulders squared, and she walked briskly toward the shopping district.

Akiko traveled, very first class, through Sasebo, Inchon, and Mukden to the little mining town. In that frontier community pretty Japanese girls were as rare as platinum. She was advanced in salary until the home office called a halt. She was showered with presents, and her passion for fine clothes now underwent a metamorphosis. Jade and crystal, silver and gold were all her fancy, but currency was best, as the panting suitors soon discovered. In less than two years matters came to a head in a disagreement as to seniority rights between the mine manager and a young engineer. Akiko was shipped back to Tokyo and fired.

Pearl Harbor had come and gone while she was in Manchuria. Akiko found many changes. The Army jingoes ranted over the radio, in the newspaper columns, and on the floor of the Diet. The antiwar Navy faction was silenced and obedient. The pro-Western bloc in the Diet was scattered and in hiding. Several had been assassinated.

The very air seemed to crackle with smoke and victory as the American butchers were ignominiously defeated on distant seas and far strange beaches. Colleges were drained of upper classmen, long since hastily converted into sublieutenants and valorously leading banzai charges around Henderson Field. The thin crop of undergraduates were all in cadet uniforms and straining at the leash for the day when they should be honored by the flame throwers' ruinous embrace in the rock caves of Iwo Jima.

Students were out and the military was in, she saw plainly, and Akiko adjusted. She invented an officer husband, recently and heroically returned to the company of his ancestors while serving with the Manchurian Army. Among the young (and some not-so-young) officers training in Ueno Park, the Little Widow of Nakano became a popular courtesan with geisha trimmings. She knew a few geisha dances and had a sweet, piping soprano. And she was adept at producing fresh-faced country girls from an apparently inexhaustible supply of cousins. This ability

[37]

did much to augment the merriment at officers' parties. Akiko did all right.

In the face of slow despair, the uneasy, half-realized sensation of defeat that preceded the acknowledgment, through the stringencies of rations, the weevils in the rice, the dog meat in the markets, even during the fire raids when every other house was destroyed by edict in the crowded sections, Akiko danced with spirit and sang with sweetness. But when the B-29's dropped their sticks squarely on the German Embassy, while just across the street not a tile was chipped from the beautiful Diet Building, she pricked up her pretty ears.

Akiko heard the story of the amazing bombing, so efficient, so infernally straight to the mark, done by giant aircraft so high they were immune from ground defenses, the whole thing done in an instant, right through a heavy cloud layer, guided by electronic eyes. She heard it at a party, muttered in drunken despair by a young antiaircraft-battery officer, and went to see for herself.

The area was roped off and heavily policed, but Akiko simply rode past in a pedicab and took one quick glance. It was true. The Diet was there and the German Embassy was not. Akiko was resigned to collaboration before the Yanks were within five hundred miles of Japan. Hiroshima and the Imperial Rescript were an anticlimax.

During the last terrible year she followed a policy of retrenchment. She collected her considerable wardrobe and deposited it in small caches with country relatives. She withdrew her savings from Tokyo Ginko and bought two small dwelling houses, one in Shinjuku and one in Nak-ano, which she rented to bombed-out families. The era of parties and dancing was over.

Much as she hated to give up any part of her savings, she found herself incapable of plying her charms in the streets. However, she quickly found a new career as a procuress. From among her friends in the outlying villages she selected young girls of some charm and promise and trained them to do liaison work in the Tokyo streets.

They were soon trained to return to her modest apartment in Shinjuku with two customers, rather than one. The income from these hesitant solicitations was sketchy, but at least she was moderately occupied almost up to the day of surrender.

Then Sergeant Hank Mueller appeared and her life changed.

5

_____

LYING now, close and warm, temporarily satiated, under the heavy quilt, they conversed drowsily and happily in their hybrid vocabulary.

"You rike me, Ank?"

"I'm crazy about you, Baby-san. Too much like — maybe little bit crazy."

"Oh, nevva hoppen! You speak compriment."

"No kidding, honest, Baby, I never had a girl like you. I like you very much — *takusan*. I like you when you make nice sukiyaki, like tonight. I like you when you wear that cute hat and Stateside suit. I like you in your kimono, and I like you *takusan* no kimono, like right now."

Dreamily, passively, he caressed the tiny firm breasts with his great hands that had learned a strange gentleness in this room.

"I like your —"

Her little whip-supple body was arching now under his hands and she spoke with difficulty.

"Japanese girl, too much small bress. American girl — all the time rike Jane russow — berry Stateside bress."

"Your breasts just like Tangerine," he said happily. He had taught her the American song "Tangerine." It had become a private nickname between them. His caresses quickened; her torso bowed and tautened under his hands.

"You speak —" she gasped.

And finally the petal lips close to his ear in the October dark — "Ank-san . . ."

The last whisper throbbed and floated in the night-flooded room before it surrendered at last to peace and silence.

Every visit — and they were almost daily now — Hank and Akiko found their ability to understand each other expanding. Most of the flexibility of their curious speech was developed by Akiko. Her English vocabulary was much greater than Hank's Japanese, although she remained reckless in pronunciation and largely indifferent to grammar. Chang no longer contributed to her facility, for she had dropped him and his attentions weeks before when she realized she could learn faster and with a better accent from Hank.

Mess Sergeant Len Whitely, introduced by Hank, was currently squiring Kiyoko to a little box-sized juke joint that had opened up in Shinjuku. Kiyoko, although still unable to say more than two dozen words in English, had gone "West" in a big way as a jitterbug. Sergeant Whitely had been invaluable in the logistics department, and through his diplomacy and pull with the Commissary officer the girls dined very well and very regularly at practically no expense to the two sergeants.

This was one of the nights when Kiyoko and Len had left promptly and Hank and Akiko had the room to themselves. Rising from the bed, Akiko turned on the light and put fresh charcoal in the big heater-sized *hibachi*. Hank rose and donned the heavy quilted kimono he had bought to combat the lack of heating in the house and they lighted cigarettes. Akiko held a Camel in one tiny hand and began to sing in Japanese.

"Hey," said Hank, surprised, "that's 'Stardust.' "

"*Hai,*" assented Akiko. "Very rubbley song. Hoagy Cahmikkel."

"Where'd you learn sing 'Stardust'?"

"Music teacher, high-school singing."

"Yeah, but that was before the war. They didn't teach English during those years, did they?"

Akiko thought a bit, a little put off by Hank's sudden abandonment of their pidgin dialect.

"Just American song. Steefin Fosser, George Geshwin, Hoagy Cahmikkel."

"Just the best, that's all."

"Damn tootin'," said Akiko agreeably.

Akiko took the steaming kettle from the *hibachi* and poured two bowls of tea. They drank, smiling at each other across the rims.

"Skoal," said Akiko merrily, raising her bowl in salutation.

"Mud in yer eye," replied Hank.

He handled the tea bowl naturally now, even turning the rim between sips very ceremoniously like a fine gentleman of Nippon. Hank was clumsy but persistent. He kept at things until he got them right. For weeks he had practiced with chopsticks on peanuts until he was adept in their use.

Akiko placed her bowl on the table and placed an earnest hand on his knee.

"If you please, Ank-san."

"Sure, Baby, what is it?"

"Very cold season. I need one suit, warm cloth like you pants. You catch cloth, please."

"You want Stateside suit?"

"I bring dressmaker. Can do very good Stateside suits. You catch cloth. Can do?"

"I guess so. Maybe after one week I'll catch some first-class cloth. Navy PX have *takusan* number-one cloth. I speak Navy friend-o."

Several times a week, lately, Akiko would bring up the subject of suits, of underwear, of nylons, of new rice, of more charcoal, some extra packs of cigarettes for a friend, a bottle of American whiskey for a very dear friend. Hank just loved to get these little things for her. It was worth it, he thought, to see the black eyes sparkle and the little coral mouth in the brown face tremble with sheer gratitude. Hell, you could keep her a week for a fin, half of what you'd spend on a small date in L.A. Besides, you could get two hundred yen for a carton of butts, and with the yen exchange at fifteen to one that was better than ten bucks. He spoke to the Navy friend promptly and kept after him until he got three and a half yards of 48-inch bolt goods of the fine woolen cloth used to make Navy fliers' officer uniforms. He paid the dressmaker, too. The little "Yellow Peril" sure looked sharp in the new green suit, especially after he got the high-heeled shoes, purse, and hat to go with it.

Lots of the men had their "Onlies" now, and they liked to while away their barracks hours boasting of their girls — their beauty, their almost white skin, their classy way of wearing clothes, their undying loyalty, the ease and economy of "shack-up" arrangements, and endlessly of their phenomenal sexual appetites. Hank boasted a lot about Akiko. He only grinned when they said he'd gone "Asiatic."

"Get smart, Wheeler, and get yourself an Only. You don't know what you're missing."

Akiko had changed to a lesser degree, but still she wasn't the same girl who came straight out of high school and went on the make. For one thing, she was an Only (only Hank), a status she had not regained since her affair with the junior vice-president of the New Manchurian Coal Company. It wasn't very profitable, just yet, but she had a couple of ideas for later. For another thing, she had grown bolder in her association with men than at any time in her preceding six years as party girl and prostitute. She had learned from the Americans that one could occasionally tell the truth and get away with it. It was the lack of concealment in Americans she objected to at first. A boy like Hank would tell you everything about himself. There were no depths and shadows in his character. What must it be like to live in a great nation where everyone told the truth? Akiko shuddered.

Still, these Americans were strong, big men — and such lovers! They petted their women before and after. They were gentle and grateful. Hank seemed to think of desire as one single experience to be shared equally, to be whetted until it was sharp as a dagger. With Hank a girl could make subtle overtures, even express desire in a modest sort of way. And such thrills! Such delights! Such transports that made exquisite tears flow from the eyes and animal cries of ecstasy spring from the throat!

It was all new — the liberty of ideas and conversation, the fine new American clothes, and the lovemaking that could be shared. Akiko found these in many ways the best days of her life, and sometimes she was almost in love with her tall American sergeant.

6

IN MARCH of 1946 Kiyoko and Sergeant Whitely decided to set up housekeeping for themselves. Akiko was ready with a suggestion.

"Ank-san, we speak, okay?"

"Huh, whazzit, Akiko?" Hank had drunk a lot of beer with the Saturday evening meal and was stretched out on the *tatami*, using the bedroll for a pillow.

"I think we catch new house. Kiyoko and Sergeant Whitely stay here."

"I dunno, Tangerine. You know where we can get a house? I think not much house in Tokyo — not easy, *ne?*"

"I have house," said Akiko, frowning into the *hibachi's* red eye and poking the charcoal vigorously. "My house before. Cousin family stay there long time. Now go back country. More big as this. Kitchen, one rooms, same-o this, one bedrooms, nice outside, a little grass, a little trees. Maybe you think small, but more better this one. No pay rent, just tax."

"Where you catch house, before?"

"Well, I tell you," Akiko drawled, in comic imitation of Len Whitely's Texas accent. "I marry before long time. My husband, he Army officer, go Manchuria, no come back. I have paper say dead, never come back, so my house now long time."

"Well, I'll be damned. You're a war widow, Tangerine."

"Damn tootin'."

"Tell me about your husband."

"I very young girl. High school finish, I hurry catch husband. My papa-san speak his papa-san, go temple, get marry, catch house. Maybe two month, then Army catch. He go Manchuria. I don't know him too much but very kind to me."

"You love him, Baby-san?"

"Not love husband, never. Not Japanese custom."

Hank rose to a seated position, legs crossed under him Japanese style, and stretched out his white muscle-roped arms, picked her up like a doll, and curled her on his lap.

"Your husband kiss you *takusan*, like this?"

"Mmm, mmm," protested Akiko in muffled denial and tearing her mouth briefly from his. "Not Japanese custom."

"He kiss you here — or here — or — ?"

"Never — ai — Ank —"

He had the habit now of watching her eyes while they clung and kissed, and he saw the long, wet, black deeps of them change swiftly, saw the dull opaque glitter come and felt her little body stiffen rodlike in his hands, becoming hard and insistent, and felt the answer in his blood, the swift change, beyond speech, beyond thought, into the vortex.

Later, when the dusk began to deepen in the room, he roused sharply with one of his brisk changes of mood.

"Come on, Tangerine. Let's go look at your house. I'd kinda like one where we could get a Stateside bed."

Four days later they were established in the little house in Nakano. It was a simple Japanese house but much bigger than the one cramped room in Shinjuku. There was a kitchen with a ground-level floor, a small iron sink with one cold-water tap, a living room exactly like every living room in Japan with an alcove bearing a scroll of art work and a vase below for flowers, a tiny bedroom just large enough for the three-quarter-size American-style bed which Akiko located and Hank paid for, and the foul-smelling *benjo*, a toilet consisting of a slit trench in the floor of a tiny cubicle with an open cesspool below.

On some kind of regular schedule the "honey carts" came and collected the contents of the cesspool and proceeded, reeking, to the fermenting tanks among the rice paddies of the Kanto Plain. Hank was pleased with the little house, but hated the *benjo*. The day he helped Akiko move, in a charcoal-burning taxi, he made up his mind that somehow he was going to install Stateside plumbing.

Meanwhile the 91st Engineers had set up headquarters in Shinjuku, requisitioned the Maruichi Building for an officers' club, established a motor pool on the very edge of the notorious Shinjuku prostitute quarter, and then, having set temptation within eyeshot and earshot of five hundred healthy young American servicemen, characteristically proceeded to make the land of pleasure *out of bounds*.

As high as twenty-five per cent of the company would be up for disciplinary action every week. The boys just couldn't stay away from geishas. In typical fashion they insisted on confusing geishas with whores, and the Japanese pimps who swarmed the streets wisely abetted the assumption. Venereal disease flourished in the ranks, and the provost Marshal, an old empire builder and nobody's fool, padded his command with hundreds of patrol vehicles and burly MP's to enforce the unenforceable. The Army medics pursued the gay spirochete and the jolly gonococcus with antibiotics and profane exasperation and just managed to hold their own. Ponderous documents traveled through the rarefied echelons of GHQ, mostly citing in military gobbledegook that it was a hell of a mess. Matters remained much the same.

It was the boys themselves who made whatever improvement was eventually accomplished. After assessing the expenses and values received from a few trips to the "district," they began to envy the "squaw men" who were shacked with their Onlies. The Only system began to spread all over Tokyo.

All kinds of young Japanese ladies were recruited as Onlies — schoolteachers, waitresses, barmaids, streetwalkers, and a few of the younger and more talented faculty members from the houses of the "district." Hank Mueller

[49]

and Len Whitely found with no astonishment whatever that they had pioneered in a major social readjustment of postwar Japan.

The Only system brought new employment to a war-devastated country. Trailing the movement came the supplementary vocations — quacks offering quick cures for venereal infections, abortionists, specialists who guaranteed to increase the dimensions of meager Japanese bosoms, landlords who hiked the rent to the gullible Yanks, specialists who cut the eye corners of the Onlies to make their eyes "Western style," beer halls complete with jukeboxes and hostesses for the stags and black marketeers to assist in the conversion of cigarettes and whiskey into yen.

Accompanying the Only movement came resurgence of the old emotions and ancient passions, true love and high romance, despair and heartbreak, older and stronger than the transient tides of conquest and defeat. Many of the Onlies were girls of considerable pride and virtuous backgrounds — schoolteachers, waitresses, secretaries — the working girls. They took American lovers only after long and difficult courtships and only after falling hopelessly and eternally in love.

Many of the Yanks fell just as hopelessly in love with their *koibitos* (sweethearts), hopelessly because they were forbidden in those days to marry them, as many of them wished to do. Others filled out their hitches and sailed for home after a casual farewell and a big *sayonara* (so-long) party, and despair followed their departure. Some of the

[50]

Onlies committed suicide in the best traditions of Madame Butterfly.

Worst of all were the married men and officers who took *koibitos* and then brought their families to Japan when GHQ lifted the ban on dependent travel in 1947. Faced with the imminent arrival of their wives and children, the married occupationaires ruptured their liaisons desperately and usually with brutal haste, often accompanied by an offer of a cash settlement. For some strange reason the finest women of all seemed to have acquired married lovers; the truest and most dedicated *koibitos* suffered the greatest shame. Many committed suicide; a few became recluses; many took to sake and prostitution after months of despair.

As for the men, they were oftentimes as deep in torment as their abandoned mistresses. Accustomed to a new quietness and domestic peace in their transitory homes, conditioned to make all decisions and reap the rewards of love and respect, they reacted violently to the domination of American wives. There was a mass rebellion and wives got "told off" by the score. Being American wives, they weren't long in discovering the source of their husbands' metamorphoses. Legal-aid officers in GHQ were swamped with divorce applications, and the taxpayers who spent thousands of American dollars to move families to Japan footed the bill to return hundreds of distraught wives to the United States.

But for the Hank Muellers and the Akiko Watanabes all

was gay and devil-may-care during the first two years. Existence in Tokyo was a kaleidoscope of humid nights, cheap liquor, fast bucks, romance and the grand passion, the glory and the mud.

7

THE new house in Nakano brought new financial responsibilities to Sergeant Hank Mueller. Akiko was ready to help.

It was Sunday under a bright afternoon sun with no breeze, following a three-day June rain. The tiles and thatches of the little houses of Nakano steamed in the saturated air. Like monster cicadas, the transport planes homing on Haneda Field droned over the housetops. Naked and glistening with sweat, Akiko and Hank lay on the bedroll while Akiko fanned them both with a small boned fan. They were spent and tranquil now, a time for slow talk, the hour of understanding.

Hank reached lazily down beside the bed and brought up an open bottle of beer and took a long drink.

"Damn stuff's warm already," he grunted, replacing it on the matting.

"What you say, please?"

Hank shifted glibly to Japanese. "I said, 'The beer is too warm.' "

"Oh, too damn bad," said Akiko sincerely. "Everything too much warm." She fanned him vigorously and mopped his body with a damp GI towel.

"Listen, one-time Baby-san, how come all Japanese girls got names somewhat alike?"

"No understand. I am sorry. Please speak again."

"You know, all girl-san names end with *ko* — Aki*ko*, Kiyo*ko*, Hisa*ko*, Michi*ko*, *takusan ko*."

"Japanese custom," said Akiko ambiguously, daring to tease him a little. Then, seeing him frown, she amplified hastily.

"All Japanese girl-san name something nice. My sister, Yōko, mean 'sea'; my name, Akiko, mean 'autumn' — very beautiful season. *Wakarimasuka?* Understand?"

"*Wakarimasen.* I like autumn season number one. How about you?"

"I love too much. Very beautiful time. We go mountain sometime autumn season, I show you. Many tree, much color, red and yellow. Someday we go Nikko, beautiful city, very handsome Japanese temple, nice number-one hotel."

"Okay, little Autumn, we'll go to the mountains when the trees are colored. Would you like to do that?"

"Oh, yes — yes!"

She was kneeling over him now to fan him better, almost bouncing with delight at their understanding. Her little round breasts with the brown-tipped nipples were firm and moved solidly with her body.

"I wonder how old she is," he thought. "She's got a body like a young girl, maybe sixteen, but she's older. If she got married at eighteen about seven or eight years ago, she'd be a year or two older than me, maybe twenty-five or twenty-six. Younger girls always bow to her first when introduced, I've noticed.

"She's got good manners, too. Likes good music, prefers smooth dancing, always picks up the best words from the Americans. Here alone with me she'll say 'damn' for a joke, but she never uses it in public. She knows rank and grades cold from a glance at the insignia. Lively as hell, too. Can't sit still a minute, and the way she bounces when she's tickled is a sight.

"That lousy, stinking *benjo!* You can smell it all over the house on a day like this. I oughta figure some way to make a fast hundred bucks or so and put in a real bathroom. This place could be fixed up real nice with those beautiful flowers and dwarf shrubs they raise over here. Only house I've seen in Nakano with a vacant lot in front clear to the street. If that was terraced on the slope and landscaped, this'd be a mighty pretty place. Take money, though, and it's costing me too much now. Aunt Mary's getting on my tail once a week because I haven't made a deposit out of my pay for six months. Wonder if I could get a hold of a flock of cigarettes . . ."

"Say, Baby, you know big black-market papa-san?" he asked.

"Sure thing, I know."

"You speak him, something make *takusan* money, *ne?* Sugar, gasoline, I dunno. I want number-one make-money black-market thing. We speak Wednesday."

"I speak Chang."

"The Chinaman? Okay, you speak — no forget."

"Why, Ank-san?"

"I need *takusan* money. Make number one this house — Stateside bathroom, no more *benjo*." He held his nose in comic disgust and Akiko bounced all over the bed with glee.

Cool air began to swirl through the drawn screens, drying the sweat and quickening the blood. He made a girdle for her tiny waist with his two great hands and held her motionless, gently, without hurting her, but letting the spring-steel power of his body flow through his hands and through her like current. And all the while they looked far down into each other's eyes and he saw the change coming — the depths disappearing, the surface glazed, hard, and brilliant — felt the muscles lift and harden under his hands, and felt each molecule of blood and flesh, churned in the maelstrom, hastening to the meeting.

8

SEATED at the desk in the battalion motor-pool office, Hank sweated out a dull Monday night on dispatch duty. From time to time he dispatched a jeep, made out the slip, and picked up the slips from returning drivers. The phone rang.

"Motor Pool."

"Lieutenant Zarnowski, Hank. I need two sets of wheels to come up to our officers' club. I'm at the Yuraku Hotel. Can do?"

"I don't know, Lieutenant. Dispatching two jeeps at once can't be done over one signature, you know."

"I know, Hank. I just spoke to Johnny Zobel. He's driving his own car. You know Warrant Officer Zobel. Put him down for one jeep. I wanta show some friends of mine our club out there. Maybe I can do you a favor someday."

"Guess that'll be O.K., Lieutenant. I'll send 'em out right away. Be sure and sign the slips right."

"Thanks, Sergeant. Be seeing you."

Hank picked up the microphone and called the drivers' ready room.

"Manning, Wunk, roll 'em, Yuraku Hotel."

"Christ, Hank, clear downtown," complained Pfc Wunk as he came in for the carbon copy of the dispatch slip.

"Whadda you care? You ain't doing anything else. Here's your slip, too, Manning. Pick up the lieutenant and a flock of his pals. Probably all drunk. If they try to get you to wind up these vehicles, quote 'em the book, and if they get tough, make me responsible. See he signs both slips with the right names, one for the lieutenant and one for Zobel."

Manning and Wunk rolled out of the pool just as a sheet of rain swept down. Hank returned to his copy of *Life* and lit a cigarette.

It was about one o'clock in the morning and the rain was slowing a little when Lieutenant Zarnowski climbed out of Manning's jeep and walked very carefully into the dispatcher's office.

"Good morning, Sergeant."

"Good morning, sir. Everything O.K.?"

"Not exactly. I was loused up by that driver Manning on the way back to Shinjuku. I believe I recognize your fine Italian hand. Did you by any chance anticipate my desire for a little speed?"

"Yes, sir, I did. Things are pretty loose around this command right now and every once in a while I find myself in a spot where I gotta make policy or get way out on a limb."

"Just what is your policy in this case?"

"Same as all cases. Vehicles for recreational use late at night between clubs — responsible for thirteen per cent of all accidents and twenty-nine per cent of all traffic offenses. I slow 'em down before they start."

Hank was getting a little worried because the lieutenant wasn't drunk, not now at least. If he was mad enough to burn out his early evening booze, he might be getting ready to burn him down.

Zarnowski's tight face slowly relaxed. He released a deep breath.

"That's a good reason. You were absolutely right. Trouble with me was I felt like a fool in front of those two Navy officers. I asked Manning to roll it up a little because it was getting late and the club closes early on Mondays. He just said, 'Sorry, it's against orders,' and I was dumb enough to argue with him. You know how chicken the Navy can get with their enlisted men. I could feel those guys criticizing the Army's sloppy discipline all the way out."

"I understand, sir. Trouble with the kids is they don't allow any room for a little discretion. Probably was room for a few more notches of speed on that jeep trip and still be playing it safe. If it was me, I'd try to make you look good and still stay within the limit. Don't blame the drivers, though. They'll handle these things better when they've been around more."

The lieutenant took off his rain cape and hung it back of the door. He laid his hat on the desk and lit a cigarette.

"Mind if I warm this chair a minute? I'm not very sleepy for some reason."

"Make yourself at home, sir. It's your motor pool, too."

"The hell it is, Hank. You know Mr. Zobel runs this thing like a drill squad right down to the last nut and bolt. Good man, too. How you going to top a warrant with twenty years of mechanics and command experience? They need a lieutenant and a warrant officer for this pool like a hole in the head. I'm lucky they let me sign my own name."

"Well," thought Hank, "the lieutenant is sure baring his brass-barred soul tonight. The bastard's got something on his mind, sure as hell, and this is the warm-up, the soften-up, the confidential-communication-between-buddies routine. Watch him, Hank boy, play him cute, now. Don't let him get inside your guard. He isn't a bad officer, but they're all bad when they move in."

"Mr. Zobel knows his job," he said evenly.

"I know what you're thinking, Hank," said the lieutenant, smiling at his cigarette tip. "I've noticed how it's going, too. He's hitting the Flit harder every week. One of three things is going to happen. He'll mess himself up, drop dead, or make it to retirement next year. Whichever way the cat swings I'm liable to have to do some real work and I'm keeping my eye peeled for a damn good number-one boy."

"All the luck in the world," said Hank, looking out over the wet asphalt of the compound.

Zarnowski laughed pleasantly.

"Okay, Sergeant," he said. "Play it cozy. I don't blame

[60]

you. That's enough shop talk for one night. You got the duty again tomorrow?"

"Yeah, I got it till midnight."

"Good night," said Zarnowski.

"Good night, sir," said Hank.

After the lieutenant left, Hank did some fast thinking — too fast. He couldn't keep his thoughts from leaping ahead, rising to the bait — fast promotion, better pay, tech., then master. Hell, he was due for tech. right now. Zobel was washed up for sure. A brilliant mechanic, he had the finest maintenance record of any pool in the Far East command, but he was losing his men. Never completely sober, he was red-eyed and mean in the mornings, mellowed slightly through the day, got stinking every night. They joked about him sleeping nights on the bar at the Yuraku Officers' Club. Of course, they'd never bust him, no matter what — just ease him out into some innocuous and harmless job where he could booze his way into retirement.

Hell, the lieutenant was baiting him into signing over. What the CO didn't know, he was extending, anyway. He was gonna build that bathroom and landscape that lawn in Nakano.

"Let's face it, son," he addressed himself from habit. Inside his skull he could hear his own voice phrasing the words clearly. The inner speech ranged out in a tiny illumined circle deep inside himself. At the edges of the circle were deep shadows and niches. Pale attentive faces were barely visible in the niches. The company of ghosts in Hank's mind listened quietly to Hank's never-spoken words as Hank lectured himself. The habit went back farther than he could remember.

"Own up, soldier. She's the first girl you ever had. You like her — you love her maybe — if that's what love is — if she'd let you. But you don't *know* if it's love because she won't let you *know* her. Real loving has to have more knowing in it. And how much do you know? You know a girl named Akiko who lives alone and went through the war here and once had a job as a secretary in an office. And she made a trip to Manchuria once but doesn't visit her folks, although they live in the neighborhood.

"But more important than what you know is what you feel. You feel she's trying to stop you from knowing her too well; even though you lock yourselves together in the night until your heartbeats collide, you must be tender without love. If you speak of love, she will stop you, and if you persist, you'll lose what you've got. So take it easy, friend Mueller. You're going to be here a long time."

9

LIEUTENANT Taliaferro discharged his jeep on the Ginza and told the driver to leave the bag of golf clubs with the guard at the Yuraku Hotel. He went into the PX and shopped in vain, as usual, for shirts of the right sleeve length, so he had a shoeshine and a malted milk. Walking to the hotel through the wet streets, he passed the row of black-market commission stalls.

He wondered idly at the Americans he saw, officers, enlisted men, and DAC's — Department of the Army Civilians — all of them with boxes, bundles, handbags, and even suitcases. Inside the bundles were coffee, sugar, cigarettes, and whiskey. He could almost tell which was which. They strolled past a stall, dropped the bundle on the counter after a quick exchange of words, strolled to the street corner with exaggerated innocence, and waited until the Japanese Dead End Kid came quickly by and pushed the roll of yen into their hands.

"The amazing thing," he reflected, "is that not one of them believed he was observed. Some one of these days there'll be some real fun with this gang. After the big operators are caught and jailed, there'll be time for these chiselers, especially officers and wives.

"Take the big blond sergeant with the bundle done in newspaper. You could see a block away it held about four cartons of cigarettes. No use bothering him — probably just wanted a few easy yen for a night on the town. But that major with the red nose was a different case. He didn't need it, and he had a big bagful — probably whiskey. He'll pick up twenty-five bucks to finance his Jap love nest and send his full allotment home to his wife.

"But the word is out to take it easy. Right from the top on down there is a philosophy in GHQ to reward the conquerors with simple privileges — didn't they fight the war? Catch the big middlemen and the indigenous racketeers, but don't embarrass the Americans. Still, some of these alleys could stand watching. Be a good place to put that young nisei in plain clothes, see what he'd pick up." Taliaferro believed in keeping files. Sooner or later they came in handy on a big case.

He winced because his wound hurt on damp days and he wished he'd kept the jeep instead of walking.

Hank dropped the package on the counter of the board shack built between the canal and the sidewalk, nodded to the thin Jap with the mustache, and walked to the end of the block. He stopped, lighted a cigarette, and looked carefully down all four streets. A dozen Americans were carrying innocent-looking packages wrapped in brown paper and cord. Some were standing before the black-market drop shacks and haggling openly. Others swooped furtively down the sidewalk, disposed of the packages in haste, and looked nervously over their shoulders as they held out their hands for the money.

The Dead End Kid from the drop shack Hank used came along the sidewalk and deftly thrust a roll of yen into the pocket of Hank's blouse. He kept walking down the street and Hank turned and strolled across the bridge toward the Imperial Moat.

He hailed a charcoal burner on A Avenue and gave the driver the address in Nakano. In the back seat he counted the bills and as usual the amount was correct. Four cartons of cigarettes — forty-eight bucks. Tonight they'd have a party — dinner at Hibiya Inn; later they'd go dancing at the Lotus Club and meet Whitely and Kiyoko. Whitely was bringing the jug and they'd drink whiskey and Cokes between dances, and some of the other fellow's from the outfit would stop by at the table with their Onlies and the girls would chatter while the men fought the war again. Akiko loved parties and she had a new outfit to wear.

Later, in the Lotus Club, he was feeling good. Akiko was sharp tonight in a page-boy bob and the black dress he'd gotten from Sears, Roebuck, a size nine that had to be cut down by the dressmaker.

"I might of knowed," Sergeant Whitely bellowed from the table clear across the room. "Crack a jug and in comes Mueller sniffin' the wind like a dog in heat. Have a drink, Mueller — how's our little Akiko? Say, get a load of that dress! You're settin' us workin'-class shack rats a bad example, friend Mueller — every Only in the goddam joint's gonna want a dress like that. Well, hell, have a drink — if you can stand Canadian Club."

"I might as well. You'll send me a bill for it anyway, Len."

He held the chair for Akiko and Whitely mixed Coke and whiskey and added ice cubes from the setup. He mixed a very light one for Akiko and a heavy one for Hank. Kiyoko had a new dress, too, and the girls immediately began an animated conversation with much fingering of each other's garments and minute inspections of the workmanship.

"Say, old son, you wait'll you see what Wheeler's got. He's really gone Asiatic. This oughta give you a laugh. You know how critical he was about Nip women. Well, I hear he found this one shining shoes under a bridge some damn place, all mud and rags, but you'd never know it now. They're out there dancing, but they'll be back and you can get a look for yourself. He musta laid out a bundle for her — so help me Christ, she's wearin' a diamond ring."

"How's she look otherwise, Len?"

"Otherwise, he says." Len addressed the air above him with elaborate scorn. "This luscious *musume* of Wheeler's got more damn otherwise in the right places than Heinz got pickles."

"I see what you mean," Hank said. Wheeler and a lovely Japanese girl were coming off the dance floor, heading for the table. "For God's sake, Len, look who joined the beachcombers — damn if it isn't the old defender of the Occident, White Supremacy Wheeler himself. This calls for explanations, Corporal. Address your superiors in a military manner and report, Corporal."

Wheeler squared off before the two sergeants and clicked his heels.

"It was like this, sir. I'm indulging in an innocent Saturday constitutional among the points of interest."

"Very commendable, Wheeler. Travel broadens one. Continue your report."

"And I stop under the Yurakucho Station overpass for a shoeshine and there she was — a livin' doll, a walkin' dream. She was low on shoe polish and usin' spit. Sergeant, so help me, she even spits beautiful."

"She wearing that outfit to shine shoes?"

"Hell, man, she was wearin' gunny sacks and a pair of shingles for shoes. But I got the eye of the true artist. Beneath her humble exterior I saw her hidden beauty, and when she spit on my shoe, it was love at first sight. Don't worry, Sarge. She don't know a goddam word of English."

"How about that," said Len. "All that stuff and silence, too. Keep her that way, skivvy boy. Conversation is overrated."

"I wonder." Hank addressed Len with grave concern. "How's he to ask for things? Some things should be asked for, I was always taught. Looks like he might teach her basic English — but very basic."

"Let's ask him," said Len. "Corporal, how you ask her for — er — uh — things?"

[67]

"I point," said Wheeler happily, "and she smiles yes at me. That's basic enough for me. Say, I'd like to introduce you all around, but all Hiroko says is 'Too much.' It's upsetting."

"I was thinking of times it could be upsetting," said Hank, while Len's great, gusty guffaws drowned out the nine-piece dance band.

"I got the solution," Hank said. "Akiko will introduce her to us just like an interpreter."

Akiko was delighted to act. First she introduced Hiroko formally to Wheeler. Hiroko's reply was a torrent of animated Japanese with her eyes riveted to Wheeler's face.

"She say you make her too happy," Akiko reported. "She afraid you go away pretty soon. She say she stay with you, and if you go away, she die pretty soon. She want you bring you clothes so she can wash and sew them for you. I think you have very nice girl friend."

Wheeler looked sheepish and hitched his chair close to Akiko and spoke to her in a low voice. Akiko talked to Hiroko and Hiroko hitched her chair closer to Wheeler and held his hand. The three of them began a low-voiced conversation, using Akiko as a go-between. Akiko was delighted in her role, bounced in her chair with excitement, laughed hugely at her own translations, and sometimes wept a little at the burgeoning love of Wheeler and Hiroko.

Hank and Len took turns dancing with Kiyoko. Len came back from the dance floor towing a slim Marine sergeant to the table.

"You'll never believe it, Hank. This here's Mac McKee

— my old gold-mining partner from New Guinea. Tell 'em, Mac. They never believed I had a gold mine down there. Did we strike gold or didn't we?"

"I did," said the Marine. "I found it on the river when I was takin' a swim, and when we had to move out, I gave it to you. It wasn't a mine, just a couple of gravel bars you could pan out flour gold. I took out a thousand dollars' worth in two weeks, just spare time. But Whitely was there two years — the old empire builder. You musta got ten grand outa them bars, Len."

"Six," said Len. "They played out and I kept working more bars farther up that paid less and less. Boy, did I brown-nose to keep from getting moved out. I fed them officers till they couldn't get up from the table. I stayed there four times when the outfit moved along and every minute I got off I tore up that river with a pie pan and sloshed gravel till hell wouldn't have it. I even got a few nuggets as big as peas outa one bar. Look here."

Len dug a tiny tobacco pouch out of his blouse and shook a half dozen rough brown nuggets on the table. Everyone stopped talking to examine them. Akiko made Len and the Marine tell the gold-mining story again and she translated it to Hiroko, who was dazed. Her Cinderella experiences of the past week were almost too much and now she sat at a table looking at pieces of gold tossed casually around her by Wheeler's friends.

Mac the Marine danced with each of the girls in turn and then crossed the hall to the line of taxi dancers provided by the management for the convenience of the stags.

He shopped through the covey of girls, variously clad in cheap evening gowns, sweater and skirt combinations, and a few in kimonos. All of them were above average height for Japanese girls. All were generously endowed with full breasts, outsize hips, and long legs. The management of the Lotus Club had unlimited candidates for its hostess staff and its standards of selection were rigidly Stateside.

Mac chose a partner so exuberantly busty that she practiced shallow breathing lest she split her gown, paid the standard fee, and brought her to the table. Kazuko was introduced, and thus balanced, the party picked up speed. The drinks were poured, the war was fought, dances were danced, and friendships cemented with Coca-Cola and whiskey.

They toasted Akiko's page-boy bob, Hiroko's dress, Kiyoko's legs, and Kazuko's bosom. They drank to the confusion of their officers and the damnation of GHQ. They proposed short days, long nights, and bigger parties. And they talked — everybody talked.

". . . and I go to grab this knee mortar for a souvenir and I find a burned Jap chained right to it."

"What's a guy have to do to get a drink around here?"

"Hiroko say please don't be angry. She don't like whiskey — just plain Coke."

"I tell you it was the Navy did us the dirty at Tarawa. We hit the beach at low tide and had to wade a half mile of flats while they cut us up like sitting ducks."

"Come on, Len-san, I wanna jitterbug."

"So this chicken colonel put the goddam map back in his

pocket and never said a goddam word the whole goddam way back to Port Moresby."

"Soon as I get out this time, I'm going back to Montauk and go fishing for the rest of my life."

"I got the eye of the true artist."

The night was spent to its convivial close with only a few minor incidents to mar the general rapport between services and nations. Wheeler got drunk and insisted he had been drinking doubles to everyone else's singles. Mac carelessly remarked that he and Len spilled more in a night than Wheeler drank in a week. Wheeler offered to knock Mac on his ass, but his challenge was reduced in effectiveness by the onset of hiccups. Mac offered to put Wheeler over his shoulder and burp him. Hank separated the two gladiators with no more harm done than a little ice water slopped on Kazuko's gown.

Peace was restored outside the Lotus Club, where they competed with a throng of couples for taxis. Wheeler was carefully stowed in a cab, the driver paid, and directions given to his shack. Hiroko was charged with certain measures required to keep Wheeler out of the clutches of the MP's. Wheeler appeared briefly at the cab window as it departed and informed the world, "I gossa eye of a true artish."

Mac and the taxi dancer, now changed into a skirt and sweater (the gowns belonged to the Lotus Club), left for the Shintobashi Hotel, noted for its sympathetic management. Kazuko yearned to visit her folks in Kure, but the round trip cost eighteen dollars, and by a rare coincidence

[71]

Mac felt that eighteen dollars was about right to encourage filial respect in a corrupt world.

Hank and Akiko piled into Len's jeep for the trip to Shinjuku-Nakano after arranging to meet for whiskey sours at Akiko's house the next morning.

"Life," thought Hank, "has hit a new high — if only the Sumida River didn't stink so bad on a hot night."

10

TUESDAY was a rough day. He put in a full day at the drivers' school at the GHQ motor pool downtown where they were training Japanese to drive all the Allied vehicles. But he got along better than most of the instructors. For one thing, he could talk enough Japanese to get by with the students. *Migi* and *hidari* for right and left came easily to him now, while most of the instructors had to consult their bilingual pocket dictionaries for every command. *Massugu* (straight ahead) he ordered confidently, *sukoshi hayaku, shitekudasai* (a little faster, please). The Japanese worshiped him. An American who used the formally polite form of address to their humble selves! And a sergeant at that! Most sergeants were formidable, volcanic in their wrath; even ordinary commands were given in voices of sheer thunder. Get Sergeant Mirror-san for an instructor and you'd make driver fast. Sergeant Mirror was a kind man and the gateway to the promised land, the all-safe sanctuary of the GHQ payroll.

Hank got back to his own motor pool a half hour late

for the duty because he'd had a flat halfway to Haneda Field with a driver he wanted to qualify before knocking off. He tried to phone from a Japanese office, but couldn't get through to the GHQ switchboard, and Zobel relieved Corporal Peterson. Zobel was waiting for him behind the dispatch desk, balefully fixing his red-eyed stare on him as he came in.

"You finally made it, glamour boy. You just had to stop at your shack for a quick jump, I suppose. Now shuddup and listen to me! You're getting too heavy on the sleeve, pretty boy. I can damn quick fix that. I can lighten you up on the left side, any time you get snotty."

"I tried to phone when I got the flat. Couldn't get on the damn GHQ line. It was a Jap phone halfway to Haneda."

"Bull shit, soldier. I could tell 'em better than that when I was a Pfc. I know your trouble. You got that yeller nooky on the brain. I've been around too damn long for them stories."

"I asked Captain Wheaton to call you up from GHQ when I came in with the flat. He should have called twenty minutes ago."

The phone rang and Zobel picked it up without taking his eyes off Hank.

"Yes," he said. "All right, Captain, yes, he's here now. Good-by."

"That was your alibi, Mueller," said Zobel. "Your nose is getting too damn brown to suit me."

The windows were open and their voices had risen to

[74]

carry clearly halfway across the yard. Out of nowhere Lieutenant Zarnowski poked his head in the office.

"Can I see you outside a minute, Mr. Zobel?" he inquired pleasantly. "I think the sergeant's ready to take over."

Hank caught the vicious swing of the door behind Zobel in time to prevent it from spattering the office with glass. Outside he saw the lieutenant speak briefly to Zobel and then turn his back and walk swiftly to his waiting jeep. He grinned as he saw Zobel slam the door of his Ford sedan and spin the tires as he roared out of the compound. When Zobel treated a car rough, he was really burned. Abuse of machinery was against his religion.

Hank settled down to the routine dispatching and checking in of jeeps and command cars and trucks. Most of the heavy vehicles were being stacked for the night as they came in. Traffic in jeeps between duty posts and officer residences was brisk.

It was still daylight when Lieutenant Zarnowski came into the office. Hank looked up in surprise.

"*Kombanwa*, Sergeant."

"Good evening, sir."

"Hank, tell me straight. You're in a position to know. What are these Japanese girls like — pretty good?"

"Why, I guess so. I don't have any complaints, Lieutenant."

"Don't stiff me, Hank. I'm serious. I've met a honey of a Japanese girl, and I'm ready to spin off my rocker if I don't get with her. I just don't know where to start."

"Okay," said Hank. "This is off the record and if you don't like it, you asked for it. First, lay off the street girls and pickups no matter how good-looking. Geishas are tramps and they'll burn you. I hear tell there's a few of the real old-time geishas in some of the ritzy houses, but Yanks never get into them. The best girls are girls with a job. If they're working, they're not peddling."

"This girl's a waitress at the GHQ club."

"So far, so good. You may have to date her awhile to score. Working girls don't come equipped with round heels."

"I'll sweat it out."

"Well, I guess that's all I can tell you. Oh, one other thing. You asked what it's like. As far as I'm concerned, there aren't any words in our language to describe it, and there are no women anywhere in the world fit to use as a comparison. It's so good it's impossible to believe."

"Your well-phrased tribute, Sergeant, does nothing to relieve my impatience, believe me!"

Hank grinned. Sometimes "Ski" was all right. A vet from ETO with a combat record and two holes in him earned on the line. The best thing about him was the way he leveled with your intelligence, didn't try to talk down to enlisted men. Too many officers tried to get palsy by lousing up their grammar and running in barracks' profanity.

"You're going Asiatic, sure as hell, sir."

"Unquestionably, Hank. But I came to you with my little problem for a particular reason. You can introduce me to the fair maiden, if you will. You see, she knows you."

"The hell you say! Excuse me, sir. There must be some mistake."

"You know Akiko Watanabe, I believe."

"I know her." The sweat under his collar was turning cold. He got slowly to his feet, holding the desk edge tight.

"Yōko Watanabe is her sister. She works at the GHQ club, most beautiful Japanese girl I've ever seen. I've only spoken to her once and only for a minute. They don't get much chance, and you know how the big brass looks at these things. She asked me if I knew you and said you were a friend of her sister's."

"Whew," said Hank and sat down suddenly. "I don't know what I thought, but I had a notion I wasn't going to like this."

"Oh, if it's too —"

"Not at all, not at all. Glad to be of service. You see, I hardly know Yōko, only seen her around a couple of times. I didn't even know she was working at the club. You're right about her looks, though. Strictly pin-up. Did she talk English with you?"

"Sure, practically perfect. You see, they have to take a course in English to work at the club or any GHQ activity. And what a voice that Yōko has! You know most Japanese girls have that tinkly little soprano singsong. This one is a throaty contralto but clear and not husky. She talks like Lena Horne sings, if you know what I mean."

"Yeah, I know what you mean. Man, you got it bad."

"Look, Hank, I came up the ladder before OCS. I prom-

ise if you can help me get started right I won't tag you. I
know what a drag an officer is on an enlisted man's good
time. It's just that I don't want to ask her to meet me down
the alley the first time. I don't want to move in fast. I need
time to talk, time to get acquainted, time to learn how to
handle myself. I thought you might be able to arrange —"

The phone interrupted and Hank took a call and dispatched a jeep.

"Tell you what I'll do. I guess it's no secret I've been living with her sister, but thanks for keeping it polite. I'll find
out which is her day off at the club and we'll have her over
for sukiyaki that night. You'll be invited, of course. Akiko
and I might go juking around after supper."

Zarnowski rose and offered his hand. Hank took it and
the lieutenant shook hands just once, looking straight at
him.

"Thanks," he said in a queer voice, wheeled quickly, and
left, fumbling with his cap as he went out the door. He
was still uncovered and fumbling with the cap as he moved
across the yard to the starters' line in the thickening dusk.

"Why, the poor bastard," thought Hank. "The poor lonesome, nonchicken, silver-barred bastard of a first lieutenant.
He's crazy in love with her after six words on the run. She
must be something I hadn't noticed. As if I didn't have a
big enough cross to bear with my Yellow Peril in Nakano.
Now I gotta watch out for him. He's blind crazy over a Jap
babe he doesn't know and liable to be careless. That man is
dangerous. Me and Len Whitely is one thing. When an officer goes Asiatic, the big brass notices things.

"I gotta keep the lieutenant clean. He's sittin' right on my future. The Army needs men like you, Lieutenant; this motor pool needs you likewise, Lieutenant; and most of all, Sergeant Hank Mueller needs you, my lovelorn lieutenant! Master Sergeant Hank Mueller, if you please — a master's rate by '48, that's the motto. Oh, I'll take care of you, you big Polack son-of-a-bitch.

"I'll take care of him, all right, but it won't be easy. That's what sergeants are for — to do the jobs that aren't easy, too rugged for officers, too complicated for the lower graders. That's me, Hank Mueller, almost number-one sergeant —"

The phone on the desk rang and he reached for it, smiling.

11

THE following night Hank had the jeep drop him four blocks from the house, because it was a fine night and he felt like thinking while he walked.

"Just an ambulatory dreamer, that's me. Damn near a wet dreamer after only forty-eight hours' separation from my little Tangerine. These lousy, stinking double-duty hauls — praise the big bronze belly of Buddha they only come around once a month. Hail, Tangerine, the bridegroom comes. What the hell am I thinking? Bridegroom, indeed. Let's keep matrimony out of this career, man. Let's take it slow, boy. Why, you hardly know the girl. Only been shacked for a couple of years. All you know is the deep dark eyes that go snaky with passion when you kiss her. You only know her skin like rich sand-colored velvet — Now, take it easy, Hank. Try to hold on to yourself for two more blocks. Remember to take your shoes off, boy. Think about something else. Now, there's a fine exercise for a strong man with *real* will power — thinking about something else when there's nothing else, nothing in all the world but Akiko waiting, and the blocks are long, and it looks funny if you run.

"Think about Zarnowski, the love-mad Pole, the passionate Polack, soon to be, if Buddha will have it, your in-law by common law. You got no right to sneer at the lieutenant, old son. You're nutty as a fruit cake. You're a long gone sucker for the Yellow Peril. You can't wait two days. How you gonna wait a lifetime? Now, there's a fine strategic problem — one too tough for the officers, too complex for privates or corporals, but just right for sergeants. You can't wait two days, Hank, old buddy. How you gonna wait forever?"

But the four blocks were behind him and it was still too big for sergeants, too, and she had seen him coming and was waiting, the door drawn back to frame the lissome child-sized shape. And he held her close and smelled the fresh-washed cloud of black hair and her soap-fragrant skin straight out of the bath. He swung her off the gallery, where she stood a foot and a half higher than he to start with, but only an inch or two higher at eye level, and holding her in close against him with only his left arm, slid the door tight with his right.

He kicked off his shoes and stepped up to the main level of the house in his sock feet, carrying her now, cradled in his arms like a baby, and all her hair hanging across his arm.

"I fix you cold *bīru*, Ank-san?"

"Later," he said in Japanese. "*Atode*."

And it was much later, a long time *atode*, he thought,

[81]

lying with her sprawled at right angles to him like a broken toy with her head against his ribs and the coarse black hair all loose across his chest. Oh, yes, it was *takusan atode* and still too tough for sergeants, and it would be a hell of a lot *atode* and never settled, forever *atode* in slow decades and long watches of a lifetime *atode*, remembering the fragrance of her hair in the camelia-scented dusk and the velvet whisper of her skin.

He set her rather roughly on his lap and sat up, looking straight into her eyes, the big hands tanned just enough to match the color of her skin, and she felt the strangeness in him this night and only looked quietly into his face, waiting.

"Little Akiko. I oughta keep my big mouth shut, but it gets too big in here, in my heart, and every girl should hear it once from a man when he feels this way — I love you!"

But her calm face twisted in sudden fear and she threw herself on him, wildly rolling him back onto the matting, and her small hands smothered his lips.

"No, no!" she cried. "You never speak love. No good love Japanese girl. Just like, okay. I like you *takusan*, but I never love. Goddam no good love too much. I very bad girl, do many bad things — please, Ank-san, never speak to me love."

"Okay, Tangerine," he said. "You got more sense than me. I never speak love again."

"We drink *sukoshi bīru* now. I wish tonight."

For the first time she took a whole bottle of beer for herself after cooling them under the kitchen tap. She brought the beer, two glasses, and switched on the light.

"Mud in yer eye," she said brightly, smiling across the table.

He saw the tear streaks on her face where she had cried in the kitchen and the two drops beside her little snub nose, the quick shake of her head that sent the drops arrowing away in shiny flight to right and left. His heart was shrunken and old in his chest as he smiled across the foaming glass.

"Skoal."

But they smiled easier as the beer went down, all six bottles he had in the house, drinking together glass for glass, forgetting the tea and rice, the problems of Lieutenant Zarnowski, the negotiations with Papa Chang, the lawn and the bathroom, walking gaily to the Japanese open-front one-room market up the block and skipping back with two quarts of Asahi.

And when the strong, sweet Japanese beer was gone, they went gravely and a little uncertainly to another market, after finding the first one closed, and returned slowly, leaning a little together as they walked and singing together Mr. Hoagy Carmichael's "Stardust" (not too loud), and carrying very tenderly a quart of Nippon beer each.

12

IT WAS easy, once you decided to start. They sat the next night over the tea bowls, and she told him how easy.

"You speak China boy?"

"*Hai.*"

"What he speak?"

"Number-one black market something very good make money, but I scare for you, maybe very bad thing, I think."

"What is it?"

She reached out a tiny fist, opened it, and the little green roll dropped in his lap. He opened it and gasped.

"God almighty, Tangerine — greenbacks. Regulation blue-seal currency. Baby-san, that stuff is *hot.*"

"Damn tootin'." She smiled.

He fingered both dollar bills, straightened them out, smoothed the creases, and laid them on the table.

"How much can you get?"

"One dollar green money catch seven dollar Japanese money."

Akiko sat quietly, hands folded in her lap, smiling a little, as one who makes casual social conversation. Hank began to rub his forehead with his finger tips, pushing the furrows of concentration upward toward his hairline.

Giving or selling United States currency to other than Allied personnel was expressly forbidden. Hank wasn't sure what the reason was, but he remembered hearing somewhere that U.S. currency was highly desired for big black-market operations and also by international spy rings. It was true you could still get practically seven for one by selling cigarettes and about five for one from retailing American whiskey, but the supply was severely rationed in both cases. With luck he could get four cartons of cigarettes a month and about four fifths of whiskey. Sugar and nylons were practically out, as far as he could figure. That left gasoline, which was a big profit item but bulky and conspicuous. Also you could smell it! Guys had tried to run gas out of the motor pool and they didn't last long. C.I.D. knocked 'em off as soon as they got started.

They were still paid in Okinawan occupation scrip every month, but the GI grapevine said GHQ was preparing to issue Japanese occupation scrip and call in all U.S. currency. He had over three thousand dollars in the Merchants Exchange Bank in Los Angeles and a couple hundred bucks of his pay stuck away at the canteen. If he could make a fast conversion of the whole bundle, he could come out with twenty-two thousand in yen. Of course, the yen was good only to spend, since it could be purchased from authorized paymasters at the PX but could not be converted back to U.S. currency or anything else. Not legally.

Still, he only needed a hundred or so a month for himself. Guys like Len Whitely and Red Peterson and a dozen others he knew would take a couple hundred or more a month off his hands to finance their parties and women. The thing was to get all his savings here in currency, exchange it, then slowly convert it back to U.S. currency, put about fifteen thousand back in the bank (*if* he could get it out of Japan), and have an operating capital of seven thousand for himself and Akiko.

But risky, and how! If he got transferred right in the middle, he could lose his roll. If someone blew the whistle on him for peddling yen around the motor pool, C.I.D. would nail him. And there were other hazards — one drink too many, one friend turned enemy, and he would be right up there at the short end of the long table — a general court.

He flicked the two bills across the table to her with a deliberate forefinger.

"Maybe two weeks we go speak you friend-o. I make plan, okay?"

"Okay," said Akiko agreeably. "You want *bīru?*"

"God, no," said Hank. "How about you?"

Akiko shuddered. "Never," she vowed. "It hurts all day — here," and she pointed to her head.

So Hank took her on his lap and told her at considerable length of the problems of Lieutenant Zarnowski.

Akiko's lassitude vanished in an instant. The black eyes

sparkled merrily and she bounced with enthusiasm. Every Japanese woman dotes on romance and thrives on the role of matchmaker. A first lieutenant and her sister! Yes, they must have a fine party, with flowers and sweet wine, an older woman to help serve. Sukiyaki, of course, and she and Yōko could practice some of their duets for the party. Yōko knew all the English words to popular Stateside songs. Could she have a little extra for the party? Of course she could.

Hank gave her ten dollars — in greenbacks.

13

THAT was a party. July 14, 1947.

Hank cut the weeds and tall grass on the little lawn. He had flowers planted, the footpath graveled, and two shrubs planted beside the entrance to the path. He paid the Japanese who did the work a dollar and three cigarettes and the florist two dollars and a pack of butts. He even scrounged a bag of lime and emptied it all down the hated *benjo* on the evening of the party.

The little house in Nakano glittered within and without. The naked light bulbs wore paper shades. Flowers framed the entire alcove; great spikes of white and purple burst from the wall vase. A lithograph of General MacArthur in a cheap frame occupied the place of honor above the scroll. Akiko's little dressing table and mirror was removed to the bedroom to make the living room larger. Stateside folding chairs and a card table plainly stamped 91ST A.E.U. BATT. stood in the center. A bottle of sparkling Burgundy, the contribution of Lieutenant Zarnowski, complete with ice bucket, cooled in the kitchen.

On the card table were fine colored straw mats at each place and the fine china with the delicate bamboo pattern. Len Whitely's borrowed record player dispensed swing music from a corner. And in the kitchen the artistically arranged chopped vegetables, bean curd, pickled seaweed, and thin-sliced beef waited in colorful rows on the platters while Mrs. Michiko Noguchi squatted on her heels outside the kitchen door and gently fanned the *hibachi* to keep the heat out of the house as long as possible.

Hank realized suddenly that he was having a hell of a good time. It was nice to have a Yank around to talk to once in a while. In some ways it had been more fun when Ken and Kiyoko made a foursome in the old dump in Shinjuku.

Zarnowski was a good Joe. And that Yōko, with the long wicked legs and the lovely bright skin, gleaming hair caught in a low knot on the nape of her neck with a high Spanish-type comb, and a smooth party dress exactly fitted to her small waist. She held a glass of wine in a languid hand and raised it to her lips at appropriate times but always put it down untasted.

But she was something! The way the little point of jet hair grew down in the middle of her forehead and gave the long white oval of her face a heart-shaped effect, the straight nose with the thin bridge, not pugged like most, and the lips, thinner than Akiko's but fresher and more sweetly curved. Zarnowski sure knew how to pick 'em, the lucky dog. Was this the face that launched a thousand lieutenants, and toppled the towers of Shinjuku?

[89]

"I'm pleased to meet you," she said simply, remaining seated and offering her hand.

"Put your tongue back in, Lieutenant. You're acquainted now."

Then the long three-hour meal. The steaming pan of oil, sugar, and soya sauce with bits of meat, onions, Chinese cabbage, bean curd, and seaweed all bubbling musically. They filled the bowls again and again and Yōko helped Zarnowski eat with chopsticks.

"Hank, this is really living."

"I've seen worse, Lieutenant."

"Hell, call me Bill. Let's have some more wine."

"Okay, Bill."

So they drank the cold wine and ate and leaned back on the cushions. Akiko and Yōko sang "Stardust" in Japanese and "Tangerine" in English, with Akiko carrying the soprano melody and Yōko singing alto. The harmony was good and their voices were sweet.

They had another glass of wine and another session of eating. The cooking process went on continuously, fresh ingredients being added to the pan as the cooked morsels were consumed. Akiko bobbed up and down to change the record player. She lit Hank's cigarettes and her own. Yōko smoked only when Zarnowski offered her a cigarette and waited calmly while he lighted it.

"This setup must cost a lot," said Zarnowski invitingly.

"You're only in Toyko once," Hank said.

The lieutenant brought up the early postwar days in the

ETO and spoke suggestively of the fast buck certain operators made in Vienna.

"Soap," he said. "You could buy half of Vienna for a truckload of soap in '45 and '46."

"I heard it was pretty loose," Hank said. "I was working in L.A. then — in '45. I came back in '46."

"I had a P.O.W. camp," Bill said. "Set up a laundry with prisoner labor. I had to requisition soap. Once I got a truckload." He rubbed the diamond solitaire on his finger and waited.

"Vienna must have been real nice," Hank said evenly. "To hell with Zarnowski," he thought, feeling the glow of food and wine leave him suddenly. "Every time a goddam officer wants to steal or shack-up he invites his sergeant into the deal. They just ain't secure without their sergeants to do the work and maybe fill in as a stooge when the going gets rough. Keep away from him, son. He's asking for support."

"All big cities are the same," Zarnowski went on. "Especially the capital. There must be a lot of loose change around Tokyo."

"I'm not anxious to get smart." Hank grinned. "The longer it takes, the cleaner my nose keeps. Try not to start me thinking, Bill. Such men are dangerous."

"All right," Bill said. "You're smart enough without pushing it. Anyway, you sure have it knocked up — girl — house — the whole setup. I got the girl, but I got a long way to go to match you for an empire builder."

"That'd be up to Yōko, I'd say," Hank answered. "My

[91]

influence ends with the introduction. Say, I gotta hand it to you, Bill. She's a dream."

"Isn't that the true word! I hate to duck around alleys with a sweet package like that. These rules about fraternization get in my way. Hell, I'd like to parade her around the Daiichi Building on my arm. I'll bet none of those VIP's at GHQ ever saw a neater bundle."

"Sweet and low, Lieutenant," Hank admonished. "I don't knock myself out over GHQ policy. It'll change one of these days. Besides, I like it out here in the boondocks."

Akiko and Yōko changed the records. They chatted in low voices while the men talked.

The meal was finished at last and the chairs were folded and piled against the wall. They pushed the table into the corner and brought out the beer chilled in ice. Little by little the polite, adult, casual speech declined.

Zarnowski had moved closer to Yōko, held one of her hands tightly, and was whispering. The room was too small and Akiko and Hank could hear the whispers. Yōko kept replying to Zarnowski's whispers with flashing smiles, but her eyes were cold.

Hank got to his feet and knotted his tie.

"I hope you'll excuse us," he said in patently hypocritical tones. "Akiko and I had plans to listen to some new records at a juke joint that just opened up in Shinjuku. Keep the *hibachi* burning."

He couldn't help stealing a glance at Yōko. She sat perfectly poised on the best cushion across the room and gave him in answer a very long, very cold look of utter comprehension. The girl gave him goosebumps in spite of her classy looks — too good-looking, too coldly correct, too hep. He and Akiko left a little guiltily.

Coming back a couple of hours later, Akiko fished her door key out of her bag, put it in the lock, and slid the door back. There was a scurrying sound in the little house.

"You wait, please, one minute," said Akiko and motioned him to wait outside. There was a whispered conference in the darkened house. Akiko came back and smiled up at him brightly.

"We go catch hotel, okay? Just one time. I pay room money."

"What the jumped-up hell is the matter with our own house?"

"Yōko and lieutenant stay one time."

"And let that be a lesson to you, Sergeant," he told himself. "Stay away from officers, you hear me? Look how fast they move in. Met your girl friend's sister only tonight and he's now sleeping in your bed. That Yōko sure didn't make him wait, either. Something tells me she came prepared. I'll bet nothing surprised her. But, oh, man, that lucky devil! What a dish! Well, here we are in a flea-bag Jap hotel and right back on the *tatami*. Hank, old son, looks like this is where you came in."

14

"It's gotta be PeeWee," he thought. "He's the only dope that'd do it and not ask questions. What a nuisance he was around L.A., always telling everybody how his good old buddy Hank saved his life, his mucking little old one-hundred-twenty-pound carcass. I should have stood in bed. I carry him to the beach at Tinian and he leeches on to me. Sometimes I think I went back in the Army to get away from PeeWee Biddiford. But he's my boy, for this caper. I can give him power of attorney and he can ship me the bundle.

"Zarnowski, my fine-feathered lieutenant, you are going to get the package and turn it over to me unopened. I want an officer's address on the package and they won't likely fluoroscope it coming through. That PeeWee boy-san, though. I never thought you'd serve your fellow man, old scout, but this is where you justify your existence. Hell's fire, that crazy PeeWee'd swim here with the loot if I told him to swim. Now to brace the lieutenant."

Riding out to the house in Zarnowski's jeep it was simple enough.

"I'm having a package shipped from L.A., Bill. It'll be addressed to you and come from a friend of mine named Lawrence Biddiford. Just parcel post. Contents one box camera, a knocked-down double-barreled shotgun, and a pair of sport boots. Will you bring it to me without opening it?"

"Sure," said Bill quickly. "Not kosher, huh?"

"It is for you if you don't ask questions."

"Good thought, shows rare judgment. No questions, Hank."

Zarnowski kept his word. He never asked. Not even when they installed the bathroom and dug the septic tank, nor when the landscapers and gardeners planted the flowers and the shrubs and the deodar hedge all around the house, nor when they had the enclosed body and the foam-rubber seats put in the surplus jeep Hank bought. And if he noticed these things and never asked, how then would he ask for the story behind the little things, like Akiko's hairdos and the fur coat that made her look like an elf-sized manikin, the electric fans in the house in summer and the gas log that heated the whole house in winter?

And not noticing and not asking, yet Bill Zarnowski always insisted on paying his way. On the long weekend in the shrine city of Nikko, high in the mountains, fishing for lake trout in Chuzenji-ko, living in purple luxury in the Imperial Suite of the Nikko Palace Hotel, and strolling high along the brawling white river, looking over the little town like a lovely legend among the restless pines. Or taking the baths at Atami by the sea and on duck-hunting trips to Tone-gawa, on skiing trips to Fuji-Hakone, over a hundred dinners of Chinese sweet-sour pork and glazed duck, in the best restaurants, over cozy dinners of tenderloin and Courvoisier brandy at the house in Nakano, he asked no questions and he paid his way.

Zarnowski wasn't doing so bad, himself, and he was a man of his word. He had a new Ford in 1947, bought at F.O.B. Detroit prices through the PX. Yōko had a new fur coat, too, a very expensive-looking one, but then, everything looked expensive on Yōko. She no longer worked at the GHQ club. And Bill didn't landscape the house they lived in. It was already done. Four beautiful Japanese rooms, completely furnished, in a quiet suburb far away from Shinjuku-Nakano, with a fine tiled bath and the *benjo* sufficiently remote to pass unnoticed, even in summer.

They kept apart from each other, for the most part. Only when they planned a trip to the beach or to the mountains, would they go together in Bill's sedan. A handsome two couples. Big, rugged, blond Hank Mueller and his toy *koibito* and lean, dark Bill Zarnowski and his lovely lady Yōko!

Both Americans were fairly fluent in Japanese by this time; both could swing the chopsticks with the best of them. Yōko showed a deplorable tendency to imitate some of the coarser idioms picked up from Americans, and these she delivered at odd moments, so sober-faced she always panicked Bill's friends. She and Bill could have won silver cups for jitterbugging. She was a flash of light in the juke joints, her long legs splintering the shadows in hectic rhythms, her clothes sheathed to her bladelike body.

Akiko had developed a liking for whiskey on the rocks, and although she got muzzy on three of them, she stayed on a cheerful plateau for the next ten, excitable, animated, bouncing in her chair with babyish delight at every wisecrack, applauding the floor show with feverish enthusiasm, chattering away ten to the dozen, getting one hundred seventy-five bucks a month allowance from Hank and salting away one hundred sixty-five without a word to her lover.

But when they came home at night, it was always the same, the one enduring, unchanging thing that was always theirs from the very first. She was always ready for him, always wanting him, never ashamed. And in the night they talked, in whispers and in low tones, of everything — of their black-market operations, of war and peace, of sex and finance, of far islands of the sea and the streets of Los Angeles, of coal mines in Manchuria and the steamboat trip to Oshima. They talked of everything but love. Sometimes Hank was a little lonely and many times he was tired of being careful.

But good old Bill Zarnowski kept his word, and paid his way and never asked. He never asked because he knew. All the time.

15

HANK had written directly to a lawyer he knew in Los Angeles and arranged to give PeeWee his power of attorney. Bill had handed him the package without comment one night, riding out to the house in his jeep.

Once inside the house Hank made Akiko lock all the screens before he opened the package. He jointed up the shotgun ramrod and picked up the knocked-down twin barrels. He placed a swab of dry cloth across the muzzle and rammed it through the left barrel from muzzle to breech. The currency slid out on the *tatami* floor like a long, segmented green worm. He rammed the right barrel in the same manner and the pile of money doubled in size. The crisp new bills lay there in fat green sausage-shaped rolls and slowly they unrolled a little, opening like evil flowers in the hot air, twenty-five one-hundred-dollar bills and twenty-five twenties.

"Good old PeeWee, he put the hundreds in the full-choke barrel."

And only then he looked up from regarding the pile of money at Akiko. The big black eyes were completely round this time. Round and strangely speculative, a little fixed and flat, the old look of lust that he knew so well running riot, but this time she was not looking into his eyes. She was not looking at him at all.

"*Moshi-moshi*," he said in comic sarcasm, using the formal telephone greeting as one who speaks across great distances. "It's only money, Tangerine."

"*Hai*," breathed Akiko in dreamy assent, "all that beautiful money — that I should see so much!"

Late into the night, they talked over plans for converting the money. It must always remain here in the house. Hank didn't want over a hundred dollars on his person at any one time. While he had been making the arrangements with PeeWee, GHQ had issued its own occupation scrip and recalled all regular U.S. currency. Possession of greenbacks was now strictly forbidden.

He cached a single one-hundred-dollar bill inside his tubular leather belt, and they placed the rest in a tin candy box with a tight cover and made a little house for it underneath the *tatami* matting in the space between the earth and the raised floor.

"First time, test-o," said Akiko. "One hundred dollar. We check, *ne?*"

"Damn tootin'," said Hank. "The Chink better come through with the seven hundred. *Takusan* dangerous business."

"Yes, yes," said Akiko. "You never speak Chang. You

never come Chang office. You don't know nothing. I catch everything, okay?"

"Not American custom," said Hank.

"What is not American custom?"

"You take big chance. Not American custom make girl friend-o take number-one police chance. It is man business."

"*Tondemonai!*" she cried. "Never."

And he could not, for once, bend her to his will. He became stern with her, a little, and put his foot down. Akiko only wept and shook her head stubbornly. In the end he gave in.

She would do all the go-between work, taking the money to Chang as fast as he could absorb it, and bringing back the yen for Hank to convert as best he might. If apprehended by Japanese police, she would refuse to talk until she could get word to Hank. He was to hire a Japanese lawyer whose name she gave him on a business card and offer bribes to the police. This, she said, must be done quickly while the number of police who knew of her arrest was yet small. Once it came to the attention of the higher-ups, small bribes would be of no avail.

But it was not likely, Akiko thought, that they had anything to fear from Japanese police. They moved only when prodded by the American MP's or the Criminal Investigation Division of GHQ. That was the real danger — C.I.D. They had plain-clothes nisei officers who couldn't be told from Japanese and they snooped around the black-market alleys of the Tokyo underworld. They overlooked, as a rule, the Americans who swapped cigarettes or small PX items for money or favors. It was the big operations they were after. Conversion of three thousand dollars in greenbacks was the big league, declared Akiko. They were now worthy of the attention of C.I.D.

That was why she *must* do all the liaison. If C.I.D. (she called them "shee-eye-dees") picked her up, she would admit only finding the money and converting it. It would be useless for Hank to get involved. He could help her more by remaining in the background. After grilling her, the Americans would charge her with the same offense under Japanese civil law and turn her over to the Japanese courts for prosecution. Until she was in the hands of Japanese authorities, Hank must do nothing, say nothing. But once she was out of the Americans' hands, he was to use all the money necessary through the appointed lawyer to influence the court for a light sentence.

Hank reluctantly agreed that she had all the answers.

Leaving Hank at the house, Akiko took a rickshaw the first time and dismissed it three blocks from Chang's place. She walked slowly, a childish, pleasant smile on her face, feeling and enjoying a sense of power like a miracle. The one-hundred-dollar bill in her kimono sleeve was a fortune. She could buy out any of the smaller stalls and shops along the street.

But one hundred American dollars was nothing. If they only knew, the hungry, skinny, clamorous street crowds, of the fortune — the enormous treasure — under the *tatami* floor. This was one thirtieth of it tonight. If it went well tonight, perhaps there would be no trouble. She must be careful and very cautious, and Hank would reward her with a share of the money — perhaps a very large share.

But she needed luck, she thought suddenly, seeing the little Shinto shrine tucked back from the miserable street. Impulsively she turned in and knelt while she prayed briefly for success in this venture. She went on, reflecting that it did no harm to invoke the ancestral gods, even if one was no longer sure of their power.

She slid back the outer screen at Chang's shop and called "Good evening" while she slipped off her getas in the alcove. The inner screen slid back an inch, halted, and then was drawn wider.

Chang's sad, heavy moonface regarded her soberly.

"Come in, little Autumn," he said. "What do you bring me tonight? A fine flower perhaps? A bud to enjoy while it opens, with warmth, good food, and a cup of hot sake from Chiba? I am in a floral mood and I will give you knowledge of the American speech for your flower."

Akiko smothered her dislike of the suggestive double talk, but answered, smiling.

"Better things than the lotus or the rose, friend Chang. I have a gift from the West — American money. It is not much, but I will have much more later."

She knelt demurely on the matting and plucked the bill from her sleeve, unfolded it, and smoothed it across her lap. She did not mention the amount, for Chang could tell the denomination of a dozen currencies as far as he could see.

"This is a very fine piece of money," he said sadly. "Do not speak lightly of an American note of such size. But you must wait while I test its genuineness. It will take perhaps an hour. If all is well with this note, we can do business with more celerity when you come again."

Akiko was immediately apprehensive. "It is not necessary to test," she assured him. "The money comes from the great bank of all California in the city of Los Angeles. I saw the package opened before my eyes when it came from the United States. It is new money and has passed no other hands — except those of my American friend."

Chang assumed an even more dolorous mien, a habit which preceded his witticisms. "What vast bouquets he must have pleasured — this wealthy American *friend* — what garlands, what nosegays, what surfeits of dew and fragrance!"

Akiko flushed and assumed her look of stricken innocence. "Please do not speak these evil things. It is true I am a worthless thing, but my friend is one with a clean, young heart. I will be true to him alone as long as he regards me with favor."

"But the test is necessary," said Chang with dour finality. "Come, give me the note," and he held out his fat hand.

"You must not cheat me, Chang-san," said Akiko, looking at him directly. "There is much more of this money to be exchanged. It is possible to exchange it elsewhere in the city, as you know. But I come to an old and trusted acquaintance, and there will be much profit for you if it goes well."

Chang did not deign to answer but took the bill and rapped sharply on the wall. Immediately a slim Korean youth came from an inner room and they conferred briefly. Chang gave the bill to the young man, who was dressed in rakish American-style clothing, and he disappeared.

Akiko sat cross-legged on her ornate cushion. She hated Koreans and distrusted them even more than Chinese. Once Kiyoko had brought two Koreans to the apartment in Shinjuku. They had enjoyed the girls with brutal haste, beaten them when they asked for payment, and departed, laughing. All Koreans were bandits!

The minutes passed with unbearable slowness. Chang continued his glum and salacious innuendoes. Was her American strong as a buffalo — demanding — insatiable? Did she not know they were world famous for inconstancy? She would be wise to keep a lover or two on the side — a refuge for a time of loneliness. He had always admired her, himself, he confessed, although many women were available because of his influence and a certain modest success in business. He suggested they pass the time more pleasantly until the test was complete. He implied that the money was more likely to pass the test if he, Chang, were properly amused.

Akiko was strongly tempted. To trade herself for an advantage was old habit, not worth a second thought, and with so much at stake it was certainly indicated. But for the first time she let the impulse subside. There was a species of exquisite pleasure in the unaccustomed self-discipline. Something was strangely changed with her now. Perhaps it was the gamble for high stakes and simple caution — perhaps it was the laughable trust that Hank had in her and the fact that he waited for her even now, worried as she was worried, a part of her desire and danger.

So Akiko smiled and parried Chang's proposals with manifest good humor and lied to him pleasantly to pass the time. Her lover was a colonel, she insisted, a man of influence and charged with weighty secrets, who worked closely with General MacArthur. Oh, yes, she invented breezily, her colonel knew the greatest secrets of even the *pikadon*, the American bomb so powerful that latest models could melt a range of mountains, but he was close-mouthed and spoke little of his work.

Chang, without believing a word, intimated that secrets spoken by colonels were worth considerable money if one could reproduce them with a little more detail and advised her to keep her ears open. Finally the Korean boy came back and nodded to Chang. Without more words Chang took a fat bundle of thousand-yen notes from his sleeve and handed them to her.

"Come again on Tuesday at the hour of the rat," he invited her. "I will take another note such as you brought tonight. Good luck, little Autumn."

Hank's end of the reconversion went better than he had dreamed. Several of the boys bought all their yen from him. Len Whitely, however, was not among them. Len had resources of his own and did a brisk trade in sugar, coffee, and cocoa. Len sold yen, himself, at times. He had a house in Shinjuku and gave Kiyoko forty dollars a month allowance for herself and the house.

Hank's regular yen buyers were good for three hundred fifty dollars a month. Besides these he had several windfalls. He met a Navy chief at the Rocker Club downtown who was setting up housekeeping. The chief had money and had just located a complete set of rattan furniture with which to furnish the quonset assigned to him and his family. Hank gave him a little discount. The chief took five hundred dollars. Through the chief he placed over five thousand dollars' worth of yen among the occupationaires housed in the same project, always at the same discount. And he made change around the fringes of the crap and poker games that flourished in barracks and canteen. The winners always bought big hunks of yen to go out and do the town.

He got to be known to a lot of the men, even officers, on Saturdays outside the main entrance of the PX and especially around payday, when the line at the yen-sales window was long. You could beat the line by buying from the tall sergeant outside on the Ginza, the blond one that looks like an Eagle Scout — wonder what his racket is.

But that was only two thirds of the operation, now that scrip had been issued. He still had to convert his scrip to greenbacks. At first there were no restrictions on how much money you could have in possession or send through the mails. But Hank found out that C.I.D. checked the money-order stubs at military post offices. If you were sending back more than you were earning, you were suspected. Hank had to send back a lot more, and he did.

He was careful to send money orders each payday for a little less than his gross pay. But he was a soft touch for the boys in the outfit who were always short. They could get money from Hank, any time at all. All Hank wanted was that they make out a money order for him to PeeWee Biddiford or Aunt Mary. A lot of the boys owed Hank money.

By the time 1947 rolled around, Hank had eight thousand dollars in his account in the Merchants Exchange. Back in Los Angeles, PeeWee and Aunt Mary rejoiced at his luck but couldn't quite understand how Hank had gotten to be such a good poker player. Under the *tatami* of the Nakano house Hank had another eight thousand dollars' worth of yen. The balance went for the improvements, the car, and Akiko's expenses. There were a lot of them.

16

Second lieutenant George Yamamoto looked about like any other well-dressed Japanese. He was somewhat above average size with an appearance of deep concentration, a man bent on serious purposes. Tonight he was rather flashily dressed in a sleek black horsehide jacket, a wine-colored sport shirt with button-down collar, a fawn knitted tie with a fat knot, high-waisted narrow-cuffed slacks, and shiny brown loafer-style sport shoes. As he steered Michiko through the crowds with elaborate courtesy a hundred pairs of black eyes whipped appraisingly over him. He looked like a man with money in his pocket — easy money — and he was regarded with envy and with the avid detail of the underfed. Here was a formula, if one could only discover it.

"These Japs sure catch on fast," he thought, as the proprietor of the Red Lotus seated them himself, even extending his obsequious politeness to the slim Japanese girl. "Or else he's suspicious. They don't waste manners on a girl usually. But then, they're all suspicious around here."

From his seat he could see the entrance to the Chinese place and he quietly marked every person who passed behind the shop doors across the street. They ordered a light meal of tea and boiled shrimp and settled down. George liked to talk.

"How's your American lawyer these days?"

"He's very kind," she said, blushing dutifully.

"Tell me if I'm wrong, Miss Sugino. When a Japanese girl says, 'He's very kind,' in that tone of voice, I always think she means, 'I don't love him, but I respect him.' Is that right?"

"I don't know about love," she said with a shrug. "It is not the same. How is it with you?"

He withheld his answer as a slender man of unusual height and dressed much the same as himself walked through the café and out into the street. When he had passed the table and was out of earshot, George said, "The one crossing the street. Is he Japanese? Be careful when you look."

"I looked as he passed the table," she said quietly. "He is a Korean, a gangster."

"How can you tell?"

"He is a Korean by his face and big feet and his nose. Most Koreans are criminals. In this district there are no exceptions."

George laughed. "I'll answer your question now. With me there is always a great wish to be in love — but it never happens. I meet a girl; she is beautiful, bashful, and well brought up. Under the bashfulness you sense the little exciting boldness. But I always talk like a professor. In ten minutes I am correcting her grammar and lecturing her on the absurdity of Japanese manners. There is no excitement in an evening of evangelism."

"I think it is not what you think. The Nipponese resent the nisei no matter what they say."

"Yes, I feel that, too. Why is it, do you think? Are we so swaggering and overbearing?"

"It is because you have escaped our traditions. You are free and have the world. We are prisoners, confined to these little islands. It is an envy too large to be endured, because you represent what *almost* happened to all of us. A little more success, a little extra luck with the war, and we might have had a world to grow in like other nations."

"That is carrying frankness to the point of sedition," he said, laughing again.

"Oh, we hated the Army — all the military. It was the wrong way, everyone knows that, but I think the nisei remind us of what we might all have been, and what we are still reluctant to become — a different people, more than Japanese and also less. One loses by changing even while he gains, but it must be done. Perhaps now under you Americans we will find a better way."

"It is the *way*," he said zealously. "Not perfect, I know, but the best possible. If I could convince all Japan of that, the whole world (at least the democracies) would adopt you in less than a generation."

"Perhaps I will find out if it is possible for me at least," she said soberly.

"Has he asked you to come to the United States with him?"

"Later," she said. "After the trials are over and he goes back to Kansas City. He thinks he will be able to get permission for me to study at an American university as an exchange student. He wishes to marry."

"And you will go?"

"I do not know. I am afraid."

He was about to reply and stopped as a movement across the street caught his eye. Instead he lighted a cigarette while he watched.

"You see the girl going into Sam Chang's? She is new. I have not seen her before."

"She is a bad girl," said Michiko severely.

"Hush," he whispered. "You spoke in English. Always speak in Japanese."

"I am sorry. I did not want to use the Japanese word, which is impolite."

"Never mind, I know the word, but how can you tell with a quick glance across a dark street? I find these smooth baby faces exciting. She is the kind of girl I preach to like a missionary when I should be making love."

Michiko sipped her tea and permitted herself a smile. "You waste your time with such a one. You see the clothes, the handbag, the shoes, and the look she gives the street before she goes inside. She will do anything for money."

They killed a little more time and then left the restaurant. Three blocks away he hailed a charcoal-burning taxi and put Michiko in it.

"You were wonderfully helpful tonight," he said. "Come in late or take the morning off tomorrow if you wish. Miss Masuda can type my reports."

"I will come at the regular time. It is nothing — please don't mention it. Be careful where you go in this district. They all know you for an American."

"The devil you say!" George was shocked into using English himself. "How?"

"By your haircut," she said, laughing. "It is too short. Good night."

Going back to his billet in the Yuraku Hotel in a separate taxi, Lieutenant Yamamoto of the Criminal Investigation Division reviewed his mental file on the flashy Korean and the baby-faced Japanese girl who had visited the Chinese. It had been a routine evening. Nothing to report, but he would remember the two faces if he ever needed to. Especially that girl.

He looked down at his body sprawled on the taxi seat. Backstroke champion at M.I.T. — the once whip-lithe frame now thickening subtly with GHQ diet and bonded whiskey — the quick needles of desire that stabbed his loins when he thought of the girl seen briefly across a dusky street. But it always ended the same, no matter how hard he tried — they laughed at him. Even his secretary, Michiko Sugino, in love with a civilian lawyer, cultivated, intelligent, desirable, and Japanese. She hadn't been able to resist twitting him about his easily noticed military haircut.

George rubbed a reflective hand over his hair and spoke impatiently to the driver for a little more speed.

The winter wheat was already half grown and covered the paddies of the Kanto Plain with a heavy green pile as they drove toward Kamakura to view the cherry blossoms in the park of the Kamakura Buddha. Hank never talked much on long drives and long walks. He liked to think while he was driving or walking. Akiko, however, chattered rapidly all the way.

"See, Ank-san. The bird scare, what you say? Farmer make bird scare like big danger bird so small bird become 'fraid to eat rice."

She pointed to the big kite affairs made to resemble hawks that were spread on wires between two limber poles in the fields. In the spring breeze the fabric and bamboo hawks leaped up and down over the blowing grain in ominous fashion.

"Scarecrow," said Hank and returned to his thoughts.

"When you gonna face it, friend Hank? This is going to stop, end, finish, terminate. No, not now, of course. You got another year to make up your mind, but you're a feeble bastard now. You won't do it. Will you sneak away when the great day comes? Or will you pick up your clothes, dig up the sugar box, take most of the yen that's left, hand her the rest, and slowly walk away? Will you pat her on the head like a useful dog, or extend the good right hand of fellowship in true palsy fashion? Or will you kiss her once more when the great day comes? And then what happens — as if you didn't know. You'll stay with her one more time and then there'll be the fine opportunity while she lies helpless and mindless, quivering on the bed. It'll take good timing — just when the tight-folded little arms relax with the last sigh, when the taut thighs slip down in repose, while the tortured bosom strains for breath and peace. Then you can go quickly with a quick, sure step far, far away to America."

"See, Ank-san," whooped Akiko. "*Kiji — kiji*. Oh, big papa-san! You shoot him quick."

Hank looked at the shoulder of the road where she pointed and saw the golden pheasant cock with his Joseph's coat of metallic red and yellow in the strong April sun and jerked the jeep to a hasty stop on the shoulder while he reached for the shotgun in the back seat. But the cock leaped high in the air, hurdled the roadside hedge, and was gone, planing away downhill over the wheat fields with a raucous, jeering bird cry thrown over his shoulder.

Hank dropped the two shells back into the glove compartment and put the gun away.

"He was sure one dandy papa-san," he said and started the jeep.

"Go away to that far strange place called home, will you, Sergeant Mueller? The place full of strangers that it makes you lonely to think of, a foreign, more lonesome land by far than this granite-ribbed hive of small brown people, where life crowds into your life, filling all the gaps, where the hard, tight arms fill the gaps in the night, as the baby-soft lips move against your lips, erasing the gaps in the speech, as —"

"You remember?" said Akiko, pointing to the carved mountain spur of the goddess Kwannon, looming now on their right across the fields.

"Very kind woman, Kwannon. *Takusan* love everybody, everything. Religion, is it not?"

"Very good religion," said Hank. "Goddess of Love and Mercy."

"But after all is said and done, Sergeant Mueller, when you have inventoried your blessings, one by one, when you have counted them by the numbers one, two — affection and kindness — three, four — passion and grace — left, right — loyalty and — you leave it there unfinished, the incomplete inventory, the half-evaluated soul of Sergeant Mueller. Because it really isn't any of your business, old son, not until you have the guts to someday complete the roster, not until you find the missing pieces. Because you can't honestly say you love her and it's practically a cinch she doesn't love you. Because you've got a stinking romantic streak and a suspicious mind. You suspect somewhere, somehow, there's more than this, more than the frantic arms, and the restless lips, and the jackknifed thighs, more than the sweat and the moonlight, more than beer and desire, more than camellias and mud."

But now they were in Kamakura, a lovely crescent of a resort city on the sea, with steep pine-skirted hills behind, and flowers in delicate spring shades everywhere among the grass and on bough and tree, filling the spaces

[115]

between the conifers on the slopes with solid swatches of rare color that drank up the light and threw it back to the eyes in waves of softest iridescence.

And there were still gaps, Hank thought, turning toward the Buddhist shrine. Only the insignificant gaps had been filled.

17

BILL ZARNOWSKI parked his sedan up the hill above the house where there was enough room to allow cars to pass if he straddled the gutter. He locked it carefully and then, as he walked to the house, he remembered the slim Japanese boy driving an old Datsun away as he came up. Good-looking kid with expensive American clothes, but there weren't many houses he could visit on this lane. You couldn't be too careful.

He slid out of his shoes in the alcove and Yōko opened the door for him. He kissed her and felt her slim hands flat against his back press him with answering warmth for a precise moment and then withdraw. He always knew by her hands when she didn't want to be kissed any longer. Her kisses were bittersweet, but it seemed as if they kept getting shorter.

"You see that Japanese boy go by here driving a Datsun?" he asked as she mixed him a Canadian Club and Coke.

"Not Japanese — Korean," said Yōko.

"Whatever he is, I don't like his prowling around. Say, how the hell did you know he was a Korean?"

"He was here to see me."

"What about?"

Yōko poured herself a Coke and chipped a piece of ice out of the top compartment of the icebox. She placed the lump of ice in her mouth and took a sip of the Coke. Then leisurely, gracefully she crossed the room, bent across his legs while she took a little lacquered box from the window seat. She tossed it in his lap.

"About this," she said, smiling.

Bill opened the box, looked at the pile of thousand-yen notes.

"Isn't that dangerous, having him come here to the house?" he asked.

"Not as dangerous as going to see Sam Chang like Akiko does. Also this boy-san can exchange the yen for occupation scrip for you. You don't like to do it yourself, do you?"

"No," he admitted. "I get the GI's every time I peddle a few lousy yen. How much does it cost to have him change it to scrip?"

"Forty yen for each dollar. It is the same everywhere." Yōko went to the record player and began to hunt for her favorite boogie recording.

"Okay," Bill said and put the lid down on the box. "Change it all and get rid of the greenbacks as fast as you can. I don't want to stretch this out too long. That's the way things happen."

"All of the Japanese money?" she asked. "What about me?"

"What about you? A new dress last week, new shoes before that, and the way you spend money on this house — I can't change it fast enough to keep this place going."

Yōko began a fast boogie step to the music, holding one hand out to him, palm up. She put a whiplike snap of her hips on the heavy beats and put in a couple of fast twirls that flared her skirt out flat at the end. She wound up with one hand on her hip and one foot advanced, cocked up on her heel, still with the outstretched palm. It always excited him to see her dance.

"Okay, jitterbug." He grinned. He took a thousand-yen note out of the box and placed it in her hand, but she left the hand there, still outstretched, with the note lying flat on her palm. "Jesus," he said and put another thousand in her hand. "Try and make it last a little longer, baby. I can't wear all your dresses in jail."

Yōko settled smoothly down on his lap and slid her hands slowly under his arms and across his back. Bill knew he'd been taken again. He was buying nothing but her body. It was all she ever gave — the same thing he could buy on a thousand Tokyo street corners for a hundredth of the price — but what a package! You couldn't get a package like Yōko without paying for it.

Later she fixed her hair a new way and asked calmly, "Where are we going tonight?"

"Couldn't we just stay home for once? We could send

out for some food and play all the records and listen to Radio Tokyo."

She got up from the dressing table and brushed his cheek with her lips as she passed. "We stayed home last night. I want to go to the Purple Peacock and dance."

"All right," he said, but he knew his old scars would hurt the next day after dancing all evening. You could never get Yōko out of a dance hall before closing time. And she was always flirting with every officer in the place, getting them over to the table, graciously inviting their Jap girl friends along and then monopolizing the men until the girls were ready to scratch her eyes out. Still it was kind of fun to see how they admired her and envied him. "You sure know how to pick 'em," they told him again and again.

Yōko, selecting her shoes, was thinking too. "The Korean will pay me a commission on both exchanges, and I boosted the yen-scrip rate up double, so I can keep the difference. And I can put away over half of what he gives me for the house and clothes. One of these days I will have enough so I can choose any man I want. It will be a colonel with eagles or a Navy commander, especially a very old and foolish one.

"But I hope he does not compare the exchange rate with Sergeant Mueller. That stupid Akiko gives him everything and is content with what he gives her for house money. It is no good talking with her like in the old days. She acts as though she were in love."

Most of it worked out the way Hank planned. Zobel got

in his thirty years early in 1948, got it in just barely before the booze got Zobel, and retired. So Lieutenant Wil-
liam Zarnowski was CO of the motor pool in name and
fact and Technical Sergeant Hank Mueller got another
rocker on his sleeve, but the big cut was on and he was
frozen in grade, not a prayer of making master sergeant.
Still, he was acting first sergeant and the pay grade wasn't
as important as it had been, and time was running out for
him.

Zarnowski came into the repair office where he was going
over the five-hundred-mile check sheets, and close behind
him came a GHQ MP and a captain.

"Sergeant Mueller," said Bill, and Hank heard the warn-
ing in his voice and stiffened himself inside as he used to
do in a tight spot in combat.

"This officer has some questions to ask you and I'm
afraid you'll have to go downtown with him. You're relieved of duty, of course. Peterson's coming over and I'll
stay here until he gets here. I want to say before the captain here that I think it will turn out to be a mistake and
that I'm going to do everything I can to prove it. Men like
Sergeant Mueller are needed in the Army and —"

"Yes, Lieutenant," said the captain. "I hope you're right
and I'll be the first to let you know. I think we'd better get
started, Sergeant."

"Right away, sir," said Hank. "Just let me finish this
five-hundred-mile check sheet — there, it's the last one for
today. I don't know what this is all about, but I'll be glad
to be of any help I can. I think those had better be filed

right away, Lieutenant, if it isn't asking too much. Peterson doesn't know much about filing. And thanks for the recommendation. I appreciate it. I'll be back later."

Hank took his cap and left with the MP corporal and the captain. The officer looked a little like Thomas Dewey, he thought, with a bottle-brush mustache, about forty-some years old, and rather mild in manner. He wore the crossed "idiot sticks" of the Infantry on his breast and no theater ribbons or shoulder patch of any kind. C.I.D. unquestionably. So this was how it ended — the short end of the long table!

His legs were stiff and prickly as they walked to the khaki Chev sedan and got in beside the corporal. There was a Pfc with an MP brassard waiting in the back seat and the captain got in the back with him and they started downtown.

But some of Hank's strength and hope revived on the ride. He was thinking straight and fast now. No dreamy flights of fancy. "Just stick to the essentials, soldier. They'll play mousy-mousy with you down in the sweat-out room, trying to find out what you know. Your job is to find what *they* know, talk a lot and say nothing. Just don't give 'em nothing!"

He knew when the driver turned out C Avenue along the Imperial Moat that it was C.I.D. for sure, and that was a good time to ask like anyone ought to do. He asked the driver.

"What have they got me for, Corporal? Popping off to that damn warrant?"

The driver shrugged and the captain said mildly, "Just some routine questions, Sergeant. I'd like it if you didn't ask any more about it until we get where we're going."

"Yes, sir," he said and knew he sounded worried, but that was all right, too. He was supposed to sound worried.

Then they were in the building, passing the armed guard in the lobby, and down a corridor to the left, and into an office with a table and some chairs and nothing else. The captain had fallen out of the group as they came along the corridor, entering an intervening room, but the corporal and the private stayed with him, and when they were inside, the corporal motioned him to a chair and sat down close to him. The Pfc stayed on his feet by the door.

So they waited.

"This is the treatment," he thought. "They'll keep me on the hook for hours to soften me up. I'm supposed to get nervous and watch the clock and start to sweat like in the movies. Well, I'll play along and get damn good and nervous and maybe I won't have to wait so long. I only hope Bill looks at that last check sheet before somebody else does."

But Bill looked at the check sheet without touching it or sitting down at the desk before the sedan was out of the exit drive. He knew long before they left the room there was nothing Hank had to write on the check sheets with a pencil. In the spaces below "Remarks" on a blank sheet Hank had written, "Tell Akiko to lam and take the money."

Zarnowski's jeep shot out of the motor pool as soon as the GHQ staff car was out of sight.

[123   ]

Downtown in the C.I.D. building Hank kept after his two guards. He worried them both with questions, mopped his face, smoked nervously, stubbed his cigarettes out after a few puffs, and paced about the room. He kept it up for about forty minutes and finally the corporal spoke to the Pfc and the Pfc left the room. The corporal sat near the door.

After about five minutes the door opened and a tall first lieutenant came in, followed by the private. Hank recognized the lieutenant immediately. It was one he had sold some yen to outside the PX several times.

"So they got you for unauthorized yen sales. It could be worse. Maybe that's all it is. How many times was it you sold to that skinny lieutenant with the slight gimp in his right leg? Either two or three and always twenty bucks' worth. Tell 'em when they ask, soldier. Straightforward and honest, that's the style. You knew it was wrong, but you won more than you needed in the crap game. Plead guilty and hope that's all they charge you with."

But when the lieutenant spoke, it was about something else.

"What's this I hear about you having some trouble with a warrant officer, Sergeant?"

"Well, sir, we had this warrant, senior grade he was, and just about ready to take retirement after thirty years, and we had a run-in several times. He was directly over me at the battalion motor pool and really knew his vehicles, especially the repair and maintenance end of the business. He was quite a man for hitting it up and got drinking heavier

[124]

and heavier. I popped off about him riding some of the men so hard and he gave me a pretty rough time. That was the first time, but I took it, and let it go."

"Go on," said the lieutenant, looking at the wall with no expression at all.

"Yes, sir.

"Well, we didn't get on so good after that. Seemed like he got meaner and meaner and he used to keep liquor in his private car at the motor pool and keep slipping out for a nip or two to get him through the day. And he hated the Japs, especially after we started using Jap drivers. Guess he'd seen some pretty rough times in the islands during the war. But I liked them all right and I went through a couple island campaigns that weren't picnics myself. You know how these Nips are. You ride 'em too heavy and they come apart, get nervous, and start making mistakes. They leave their emergencies on and get the bands smoking and race the motors and get jumpy with the clutch and then they kill the engine. Zobel — that was this warrant's name, Mr. Zobel — he'd have a good excuse to ride 'em even worse and there was no end to it. So one day we had it. I told him he was a goddam lush and a lot of things I maybe shouldn't. I remember I said he mighta been a good man once, but he was a has-been now, and why didn't he hurry up and kill himself with booze so the rest of us could get some work done? He took a swing at me in the dispatch office, but I just caught it with my arm, and he stopped trying to fight after that one wild punch."

"What'd he say to all this?" the lieutenant asked, lighting a cigarette.

"Well, he said quite a lot. I don't remember everything, but he called me a yellow-striped shack rat and a brown-nosed suckholing bastard, and said he'd rather see a man drink himself to death than do what I was doing."

"What did he mean by that?" For the first time there was a little extra touch of interest in the officer's tone.

"Well, sir, you see, I knew some Japanese girls and I used to bum around Shinjuku with 'em nights and he hated Japs, so I suppose that's what he was driving at. That's what he meant when he called me a shack rat."

"I see," said the lieutenant, blowing a reflective jet of smoke through his nose and looking out the window, and then he faced Hank and said evenly, "You recognized me the minute I entered this room, Sergeant."

Hank waited a minute. He had known this was exactly the way it would be. "Get me talking, rattling along, build up a little feeling of security, and then give me the harpoon. Well, I'm ready for you, cop. I got a feeling you and I are going to go round and round many a long summer's day."

"Yes, sir, I did."

"Why? Where have you seen me before?"

"On the Ginza outside the PX."

"You remember what happened on those occasions?"

"Yes, sir. You bought some yen off me, twice, I think. Twenty dollars' worth each time. I took the scrip and gave you the yen."

"You sold other people yen on those occasions. How many?"

"I don't know if I remember exactly, but about six to eight persons each time. I had over a hundred dollars to get rid of each time."

"You know the regulations governing yen sales and purchases?"

"Yes, sir."

"Where'd you get this load of yen, Sergeant — in a poker game?" The phrase about the poker game was thrown out with a noticeably curled lip.

"No, sir, in a crap game. Several crap games."

"You got lucky, I take it."

"Not much, sir. I didn't win much actually making passes. I mostly faded other guys and bet with the dice. You see, they get a load of yen and they bet more reckless 'cause they don't really think of it as money, it being so much cheaper than our money and all. So if you offer 'em a bet, lots of times they don't stop to figure the odds and they cover. I got most of it that way."

The lieutenant didn't say anything for a long time. Pretty soon a nisei second lieutenant came in and laid some papers in front of him. The interrogator asked a low question and the nisei second john flipped a page and pointed to a line and the questioner nodded.

"Tell you what, Sergeant. That's a pretty story you've told here today. I especially liked that touch about the crap game. I'd like to find one that easy, but I'm not lucky like you. But" — and he sighed ironically — "that's your story, and I'm sure you intend to keep telling it to me, so we'll listen again tomorrow.

"I'm going to return you to duty. You're technically under arrest and charged with violation of military regulations in connection with the sale and purchase of yen. You can work with the motor pool and come down here until we get this business settled. We'll start taking testimony next time. I'll arrange your schedule of interrogation with your CO. You are restricted to your work area and your barracks. If you violate this order, I'll have you confined in Sugamo Prison and placed under guard. Understand?"

"Yes, sir."

"Take him back now, Corporal."

He didn't talk to the MP on the way back. There was just the two of them. Zarnowski was waiting in the dispatch office.

"How was it, Hank?"

"Easy the first time. I'm restricted to duty quarters, but not under guard. We're going to go around for another waltz tomorrow."

"What was the beef? Yen sales?"

Hank nodded.

"Get my message to Akiko, Bill?"

"I was there before you made six blocks. She wouldn't listen, though. Played dumb. Doesn't know about any money, she claims, and she won't run. I had a funny feeling she's thinking of turning herself in as a sort of sacrifice if things get too tough. We'll have to kinda watch that girl."

"Jesus, Bill, I don't dare go near her. They probably got a man staked out to see if I violate my yard parole and watch where I go. I'll have to ask you to sit on her as much as you dare without getting involved. The one thing she mustn't do is go near those guys. There's a fifty-fifty chance I'll get a light rap if they can't prove anything but yen sales."

"I'll stop again tonight. I'll try and get her to come over to our house and stay with Yōko until this is over."

"Thanks, Bill. Well, I might as well be working. I'll go in the shop and see how the greaseballs are coming on that six-by."

18

AFTER the first two or three days they only brought him down for interrogation after supper. There were three of them — Captain Wentland, who had accompanied him on the first trip in the staff car, Lieutenant Taliaferro, who did most of the interrogation and to whom he had sold yen on the Ginza, and Second Lieutenant George Yamamoto, the Hawaiian-born nisei. The interrogation lasted for eleven days, and if they hadn't told him, he'd never have known he was under arrest. Outside of the first day he was never threatened with confinement or warned against leaving his work area or barracks. It seemed to him they were waiting for him to make a move. He waited.

Taliaferro was plodding, slow, completely imperturbable; a former lawyer with the Wisconsin Tax Commission, he had an unvarying formula. Ask questions and let 'em talk, the more the better. Ask each question in at least four different ways, and if you haven't gotten what you want, start over. Every few interviews the pace would change sharply, with Captain Wentland taking over. He began by being deceptively mild, rather patronizing and kindly, with a sort of boys-will-be-boys attitude toward the wayward sergeant. When he didn't get what he wanted, he became the Menace, transfixed the suspect with a glittering eye, shot questions like thunderbolts, and eventually pounded the table and bellowed with Jovian wrath. Yamamoto only took over toward the last. He was the best of all and consequently the most dangerous — sympathetic and understanding, even enthusiastic, agreeably diverging on any subject at all, talked more than he interrogated, and flattered Hank's intelligence.

After the first day there was a DAC secretary acting as recorder, but half the time she didn't even take notes, Hank suspected. They were after something big, bigger maybe than he could possibly be guilty of. At times he thought he might have been a link in some monumental act of treason in which his money exchange had played an incidental part. Things didn't add up. No one at the motor pool knew he was under technical arrest. Zarnowski might have requested his parole on promise to produce him when wanted, but Bill insisted he had never discussed it with anyone or been approached after the first day. He couldn't find any obvious tail covering his movements, but assumed it would be one of the enlisted men, planted in the barracks, unknown to him.

He learned a little, not much, but something, from the questioning. Did he know Chang Ho San, a Chinese merchant in Shinjuku? A Cantonese sometimes nicknamed

Sam Chang? No, he knew no Chinese by any names. How about a Japanese national named Matsuo Higuchi? Anyone called Mike Higuchi? A flashy-dressed, rather tall for a Jap, half Korean named Mike? How about a certain house in the Ueno district? Ever go to a Ueno whorehouse? Did he know a restaurant near Ueno Station called the Red Lotus? No, Hank didn't know Mike or the Red Lotus, either.

Nights in the barracks he was almost gay, caught up on his reading, played a desultory cheap game of poker, cracked wise, and did a lot of thinking.

"The Chink is the one Akiko peddled the greenbacks to, of course. They want him, but they haven't got him. This Mike they got, the Ueno flash. He must have been a go-between for the Chink and they need a little more than they can shake out of him. But how come they skip to me? They couldn't pick me up, at least I doubt it, just for yen sales, and then try to link us up by association. It doesn't figure. Too many guys sell yen. To come to me they'd trace back through Akiko and she'd be in it with both feet. But I can't find out if they're grilling her down there and I don't dare go near her. Maybe they've searched the house and found that roll of yen under the *tatami*. The poor kid probably thinks I've run out on her."

Zarnowski couldn't tell him much. He had tried to get Akiko to come and stay with Yōko, but she had refused. She wouldn't tell him if she was being questioned or not. She wouldn't leave town and hide in the country, and she didn't know anything about any money, Hank's or any-one's. She acted, Bill said, as though she didn't trust him.

[132]

"Bullets," said Hank and flipped his ace out of the hole.

"You had it," said Pearson and threw in his stud hand while Hank piled up the chips. "You're a regular heller for hands that don't read, ain't you, Sarge? Someday your luck's gonna run out on you and I'll be around."

Suddenly Hank knew. It was Pearson, the replacement Pfc, always in the barracks every night with Hank. Always coming in just a little before Hank would return from downtown after a session at C.I.D. Pearson was the tail, and he suddenly felt better. It helped to know who you had to go around.

Something happened on the tenth interview. He was on his way downtown with the MP corporal in a plain GHQ jeep and the corporal wasn't even wearing an MP brassard any more. Just as they turned into C Avenue after waiting out a traffic light they were passed by another jeep with the MP white star on it and there was a little Japanese girl in front. It was Akiko, and she saw him just as he recognized her, and gave just the slightest shake of her head without any change of expression.

Hank went into that interview with a whirling head. What did she mean by the shake? Probably meant not to talk, to continue to deny, and she would do the same. But was it maybe a gesture of despair, meaning, "I tried to hold out, but I couldn't?" Some way he was going to find out, if he had to murder Pearson.

Oddly enough the interview that day was more enlightening. Hank drew the captain. That meant they were get-

[133]

ting impatient. The bulldog was coming with bared teeth and fairly scattering bolts of determination. Wentland was the best in some ways. It was easy to get him riled and then sometimes he spilled a little. When he thought of little Akiko crouched on the edge of one of those hard chairs, he felt like being a stinker to Wentland. But probably Lieutenant Yamamoto would be questioning her in Japanese. That wouldn't be too bad, especially if it was the first time.

So he answered Wentland as the captain reviewed some of the old ground, and he answered a little wearily, a little insolently, and it took only a few minutes. The good captain's color kept rising up out of his shirt collar, and pretty soon his voice was rattling the window panes and the little capillaries in his nose stood out in violet bas relief.

"Oh, you are, are you? By God, Mueller, what the hell do you think this is, a goddam picnic? You're in so damn deep you're never gonna come out of a federal pen, and the sooner you realize it, the sooner we'll quit this goddam playing around."

"I'm still getting tired of it all, Captain. You know perfectly well, sir, you have to charge me in order to interrogate me like this. I've just been doing you boys a favor by going along with this investigation, and you still haven't made a charge. I'm guilty of the yen sales and I'll admit it and pay the penalty, but you can't throw a general court at me for that."

"The hell I can't. I can throw a general at you for talking to me like you're doing right now. And, by Christ, if you want more charges, you can have 'em. How about a charge of running ten thousand dollars' worth of green-backs through the black-market money exchange? Hey, how about that? How about being the source of supply by which a Chinese Red outfit gets itself a bundle of perfectly good U.S. currency for use in espionage work? That big enough to suit you, Mueller? How about a friend of yours named Lawrence Biddiford and your ex-prostitute Japanese girl friend Akiko Watanabe? How'd you like her brought up on a war-crimes charge? We can prove her an old Jap Army collaborator from way back. Listen, smart boy, you want charges, I can give you charges you haven't dreamed of —"

The captain ran completely out of breath and coherence. If he hadn't been so carried away by rage, he'd have seen the startled look on Hank's face when he mentioned the ten thousand dollars of currency. But Hank recovered from his shock in time. He didn't especially mind the reference to Akiko as a prostitute. She had told him enough of her prewar career for him to suspect that it was close to the truth. He had decided a long time ago it didn't make any difference. What was important was that the C.I.D. had tied them together all along. He had to see her. He had to see her that night!

That night in the barracks he took three of the big capsules of phenobarbital, known to Army medics as Yellow Jackets, from his foot locker and put them in his shirt pocket. It was a Saturday night and the barracks were too empty for a poker game, so he got to his feet and punched Pearson on the shoulder.

"Get off it, soldier. Let's go over to the canteen and get a Coke. Seein' you're so generous with your poker money, I'll make you a present of a cold Coke."

He walked out of the barracks without waiting for an answer and Pearson followed him. Pearson always followed him. Inside the almost deserted canteen he put two nickels in the dispenser and caught the icy bottles as they slid out of the slot. He was afraid the gelatin wouldn't dissolve fast enough in the cold drink, so with his back turned to Pearson he popped one capsule in his mouth, bit through it with his front teeth, and opened one Coke bottle. He took a greedy swig, rinsed the bitter phenobarbital with the mouthful of Coke, and spat the contents back into his bottle as he faked a second swig. He opened a bottle and handed it to Pearson.

"Watch Buttercup trying for that three-cushion bank," he said, gesturing toward the pool table with his bottle of Coke. "I got a dollar says he does."

Pearson looked at Buttercup, an apple-cheeked corporal with platinum hair who was something of a dud at pool but had ambitions of being the canteen shark.

"It's a bet," said Pearson and led the way to the side of the table facing Buttercup. He set his Coke down on the rail and figured the bank in reverse. By this time Hank had chewed and spat two Yellow Jackets into his bottle. The filthy taste of the phenobarbital was so strong he was afraid to swallow, and every time he thought Pearson wasn't looking he spat into his handkerchief. He swished the bottle slowly and swapped bottles with Pearson simply by placing his own next to Pearson's Coke on the rail and then coaxing Pearson's bottle around his bottle and into his hand with his long fingers.

Buttercup shot and missed.

"Pay at this window, sucker," said Pearson and Hank paid cheerfully.

"Funny, I just felt lucky tonight. But, hell, I never was right on hunches, Pearson. Your good health, sir."

He raised and drank and Pearson drank half the bottle.

"I gotta get him outa here and back to the barracks. He'll start to fold in three minutes with that charge in him, and it can't happen here, old son. It can't happen here."

He finished his Coke and Pearson took another swallow and left a third in the bottle.

"Christ, Hank, the Cokes you buy taste like old jock-straps."

"I didn't know you was a collector, buddy. Let's go back and play some two-bit showdown. I spend a prince's ransom on you and that's the thanks I get."

Pearson was getting cute as they walked back, trying his hand at the boy-detective role.

"How come you're such a barracks hound, Hank? The boys tell me you're General MacArthur's number-one skivvy boy."

"I got trouble, chum, big stuff. Way over your head, but I gotta talk to somebody."

They were in the dark now, halfway across to the barracks, and Hank began to tell him. He told him the truth. He might as well. The stuff was inside of Pearson, so what the hell.

Hank left Pearson already deep in blubbering sleep in a screen of bushes close to the barracks, packed a musette bag with toilet articles and some shotgun shells. He took the shotgun in the takedown canvas case from his foot locker and went out fast. He walked straight to the motor pool, crossed the compound, and found the wall beyond the parked heavy trucks. He stood on the radiator of a six-by-six, parked bumper to the wall, and climbed to the hood, laid his two bags on the wall, and he was loose in Tokyo. Ten minutes of back alleys took him to Z Avenue and a charcoal-burning taxi. He left the cab some distance from Akiko's house and reconnoitered it carefully from all sides. Finally he came on his belly and elbows across the terrace to the kitchen door and rapped. He heard Akiko coming and put his mouth against the screen.

"Akiko. This is Hank. Hurry!"

Akiko unlocked the kitchen screen and stood back out of sight while he slipped in. Then she hurled herself into his arms.

"Ank-san. I am sorry — so sorry. No good for you. I dumb Japanese girls, make you big trouble."

"Don't cry, Baby-san. It's no use. I think maybe we can make everything O.K. now. Must talk *hayaku*."

"Okay," she said and the two round tears which had slid just to the edge of her cheekbones she flipped to right and left with a quick double shake of her head. She faced him, smiling.

"Listen, Akiko, how many times you speak with C.I.D. man?"

"Three time speak. Lieutenant Yamamoto, nisei officer. Two time speak Japanese police. Lieutenant Yamamoto very kind, not say many bad thing. Japanese police very bad, *takusan* say bad thing. Sometime punch!"

She gestured toward her jaw with a slapping motion and Hank saw her bruised and swollen face.

"The bastards. We'll stop that, dearest. We're buggin' out, you and I. Come on, honey, get your clothes. We go country, go mountain long time."

She looked at him strangely with her bruised cheeks wet and her eyes suddenly sad and soft. He had called her "dearest" and Akiko knew what it meant!

"Okay," she said and began to pack a bag.

"How about Japanese money? C.I.D. catch?" He gestured toward the corner of the *tatami* mat where they kept the hoard of yen.

"*Takusan* look, one day. Same day come back-o Japanese police, *takusan* look. No catch. I take country before. Money now cousin house, O.K. We catch pretty soon."

They left the house in the dark and Hank picked up the musette bag and the shotgun from the bushes on the terrace. After a few blocks they picked up a cruising taxi, a gasoline-burning Chevrolet this time. Akiko directed the driver to a station clear across Tokyo in the Asakusa district which was completely unfamiliar to Hank. He waited in the cab while Akiko consulted the train schedules inside and then they went to a teahouse nearby and dismissed the taxi. They sat for an hour and a half, drinking tea and nibbling *sushi* and holding hands like high-school kids while they talked.

"You poor kid. What'd they ask you?"

"All the time same thing. How much greenback money you touch. I say nothing. They say how you catch money for Stateside clothes, how you fix house, no work, *takusan* spend money? I say my boy friend give me house money, very kind, present clothes, never touch American money."

They were in a curtained booth and suddenly she twisted around the tiny table and hurled herself against him, crying wildly.

"They say you die, Ank-san," she sobbed. "Japanese police say American Army will court-martial and take you Sugamo Prison, and you be dead."

He comforted her tenderly, whispering silly little loving phrases. He held her close and kissed the tears, his heart so swollen it hurt. They sat very close; the heat of their bodies mingled until their clothes were wet against their skins. She kept stroking his sleeve and his breast and making fierce little clutching motions as though to convince herself the flesh beneath the khaki was real.

But for the first time he knew no passion. They looked deep in each other's eyes with a sweet new sharing that was somehow dedicated beyond the frenetic flesh, compassion that transcended ecstasy, and in their new love were sadness and bitter knowledge. For they were caught, trussed, and delivered, beyond any hope. It was only a matter of time. But Hank and Akiko knew quite clearly and quite hopelessly it was going to be the best time and they could only try to make it last.

19

ALL Hank could tell was that they were headed roughly north or perhaps northeast, probably on a course crossing the base of the Chiba Peninsula, for most of their excursions out of Tokyo had been made in his jeep or Zarnowski's sedan. Earlier he had made trips, mostly south of Tokyo and Yokohama, by the RT, the electric railway, and this was his first ride in a Japanese steam train. He didn't know if there was an Allied car on the train — the special car for occupation personnel only, with comfortable seats and clean floors — but even if there had been, it would have been the last place he would have gone. He and Akiko hung on overhead handrails as the little locomotive jerked the few mixed freight and second-class passenger cars through the night. He felt as conspicuous as a neon sign, with his great height and bulk towering over the jam-packed Japanese in the dingy coach with the grime-crusted windows and filth-layered aisle.

"Oh, you'll learn what it means, old son," he told himself. "You'll get to know the people now, my fine fellow.

You'll really enter into the community spirit, as they say. For this puts you beyond any necessity of courtesy, any deference to your disgraced uniform, beyond all privilege. You've abdicated all the prerogatives of victory. Maybe now you'll learn how it feels to be a Jap, after you've eaten a thousand meals of fish and rice, smelled their sweat and caught their lice on a hundred packed second-class coaches, slept with a log for a pillow, and paid five yen for a rare bath where you share the water with the whole damn village."

They rode on through the night with frequent stops at stations every few miles. They were afraid to talk either English or Japanese, for in the coach they had so little privacy that the breath of their neighbors was no sooner exhaled than it was gathered into their lungs undiluted. Akiko was unable to maintain her hold on the high overhead rail after a few miles and finished the ride clinging to Hank's arm. It took three and a half hours.

"And pride, too," he thought as they pitched and braced to the cataleptic motion of the train. "How about pride, ex-sergeant? Especially her pride, not yours, for you have abdicated that way back, in the beginning. How does she feel, a Japanese woman of a certain intelligence, hanging to a great lump of an American dogface, surrounded by the eyes of all Japan? For she's marked a thousand ways with the stamp of the horizontal collaborator, the whore with the page-boy bob, the prostitute in the Stateside suit, the nylon stockings, the painted mouth.

"You can't see it, no matter how you look at her. She

clings to your arm without fear or visible embarrassment. She looks straight in your eyes and smiles unashamed, and she knows better than you ever will that she's a monument of unmentionable shame every foot of the way — through every street you've ever walked, into every juke joint and restaurant, the target of a million black shoe-button eyes.

"Oh, we'll talk about it now in whatever hovel we hide in, while we scurry like frightened animals through the bamboo groves. We'll never stop short of the mark again, afraid to name the name of love. I'll make you know love by its number-one name, poor girl. There won't be much time before they hunt us out of the boondocks, beloved. But for that little time I'll wear my heart on my sleeve for you, little Akiko. Sweet streetwalker, named for autumn and all its lovely sadness, I'll love you now — my consort in folly — my bride of hopelessness."

As the train lurched into a station marked ONA they stepped out in a jostle of passengers onto the platform and found themselves in a sleeping city among great hills of groves and grass now black and gilt with summer moonlight. Akiko led him to a nearby stall front, pounded sharply on a sliding door, and after some staccato exchange with a woman inside, a man appeared, pushing a motorcycle taxi with a two-passenger cab over the two rear-drive wheels. They climbed into the cab, clutched their packages, and proceeded for some minutes to the outskirts of what Hank judged to be a town of six or seven thousand. The cab stopped before a neat two-story house with tile roof rather than thatch, indicating a certain social stratum, and Akiko made the driver wait while she went in. The motorcycle taxi driver hadn't spoken a word since he had come out of the shop near the station, and Hank offered him a cigarette while they waited. The driver bowed from the seat, grinned gratefully, and made a mewing noise as he placed the cigarette behind his ear for more leisurely consumption. Hank realized then that he was a mute.

There was a long wait and Hank heard snatches of low-pitched conversation inside the house; there was some stirring of feet and light in an upstairs room. A man grumbled and Hank heard a sharp questioning tone from the man several times. Then the light went out and Akiko came back to the cycle cab and climbed in.

"Okay now," she said. "We have money to live."

Conversation was as impossible as comfort in the cab, which bounced more viciously by far than the train. The driver traveled on progressively worse and worse roads. At times he seemed to be following a pair of narrow ruts on top of a grass-grown dike between flooded rice paddies. Brush swept the sides of the cab along the trails. Then more roads with great chuckholes, then a gravel road, then more diketops, finally a better road, cobbled streets, and another town. It was the longest ride Hank had ever taken in Japan without passing through a single settled community, but he judged the mute was sticking to back roads on orders from Akiko. At last they arrived at a country hotel where Hank could smell the sharp weedy odor of the sea mixed with the rancid reek of fish. The hotel proprietress took

[145]

their shoes, issued them slippers, led them to a large second-floor room, and brought tea. It was getting daylight outside the paper screens when they finally slept exhausted on the floor bed, still holding each other a little fearfully with clutching arms.

20

Down in C.I.D. Headquarters on C Avenue there was less consternation than might have been supposed. In fact, after the situation was evaluated, there was even an element of satisfaction.

"I'm going to hate to lay this file before the Colonel," said Captain Wentland, "but I intend to tell him I was responsible. In the first place, I agreed to George's idea of leaving him uncharged and under surveillance. In the second place, I picked a dope for a tailing job. But I think I can point out that this sews up the case, and when we get our hands on him again, we won't waste any time."

"It occurred to me," said Lieutenant Taliaferro, "that I started out by underestimating Mueller. The longer I talked to him the more I realized he was a pretty smart kid. He wouldn't yield an inch until he knew which way the questioning was heading. Funny, for a kid with a clean record up to this time, he made a damn slippery witness. I agree we'd have had a tough time hanging the greenback charge on him unless the girl cracked later. We won't now."

"That's right, Captain," said Yamamoto thoughtfully. "We don't have to make much of an effort to chase him. It isn't as though we hadn't seen men run for the brush before to beat charges. They always come out, hungry, dirty, and sick, or just lonesome for movies, juke joints, and their own language. None of them last in the out-country."

"The way things are right now, we can't waste an extra man on him," said Wentland. "The usual wanted report has gone to all area commands and the Jap police are following up on the Watanabe woman. You know about this situation at Kobe, well, we're going to have our hands full with that. If I can get the Colonel to agree, we'll give him a mile of rope and someday an MP will pick him up gorging on hamburgers and ice cream at the Ernie Pyle."

"We still got that Los Angeles report," said Taliaferro. "You suppose we oughta ask 'em to work on this Biddiford and Mueller's aunt?"

"Nothing to be gained that I can see," said Wentland wearily. "He gave his friend power of attorney and the friend withdrew his savings from his bank. We can't even prove conclusively that Biddiford shipped the money to Mueller. The post office records here fail to reveal anything like a money order or a series of them covering ten thousand dollars. It probably came in a parcel post package. He got a lot of them, mostly from mail-order houses in L.A., clothes for his girl, I suppose."

"One more thing, Captain," said Yamamoto. "I'm convinced that *three* thousand dollars was Mueller's whole roll. The rest of it came from someone else. This Watanabe girl was significant by what she didn't say. Of course she denied everything from the first question. I suggested it might have been as much as three thousand and she showed no surprise. I got the impression she was conditioned to expect that was the amount that would be mentioned. But when I suggested the second day the amount might be ten thousand or more, her hat nearly fell off."

"Jesus God!" cried Wentland. "You mean we got another nigger in the woodpile?"

"That's my belief," said Yamamoto precisely.

"Now listen, both of you," said Wentland after a moment of thought. "Get this Mr. X out of your heads. We just can't get the men to run it down. This Kobe situation is a hell of a mess. You start investigating light colonels and you can't afford to bitch it. There's another matter coming up shortly in Hokkaido that's too serious to even talk about right now. As far as this file goes, Mueller's our boy, and when we get him, the case is closed. All right, gentlemen, I'll see you Monday."

The little fishing village of Omikura lies on a small harbor that indents the very apex of the Chiba Peninsula, its bright crescent of water clasped in two crablike dikes of volcanic rock, and through the narrows the tide makes menacing music as it fills and drains its rocky cup. Behind the town rise steep eroded hills terraced into rice paddies and vegetable fields, but occasionally the granite skeletons

[149]

of ancient mountains show through the thin flesh of the soil on the steeper slopes and outcrops. The skulls of the hills are crested with sentinel pines, twisted and tortured by the Pacific gales, and the worst slopes and ravines, beyond any possibility of agricultural use, are choked with osiers, bamboos, and smaller brush resembling sage. Through the town and into the harbor flows the Warimakawa, a placid, meandering river affected by moderate tidal bores for half a mile upstream. Beyond that point the river can be seen dropping in bright reflections from still higher hills.

On the narrow strip of dark volcanic sand Hank and Akiko walked to find a rock sufficiently remote from the clusters of men and women reeling nets and mending boats about the shore. They sat smoking and looking out over the sea where the blue sharpness was now softening in the midmorning heat, and turning to look with lively delight at the encircling hills, with the ones farthest inland swimming in cobalt haze.

"One thing I worry," said Hank, taking a cigarette from her. "The C.I.D. men say maybe Sam Chang catch ten thousand dollars. You believe?"

Akiko nodded thoughtfully. "*Hai*, I think it's true."

Then she was silent a moment and let her eyes slant expressively as she gave him a quizzical sidelong glance.

"You know?" she asked meaningly.

"No, I don't know. Who was it?"

"I think Yōko-san teach Lieutenant Zarnowski money business. I think lieutenant catch seven thousand dollar, give Yōko. She make big money business with Sam Chang."

"Like hell! Did Yōko know about you and Sam Chang?"

"Yōko know Sam Chang before. She catch *takusan* cigarette present from many officer GHQ club, and all the time take Sam Chang for money. Yōko very beautiful girl, but *takusan* have black heart. She want *takusan* money. Yōko-san *takusan* butterfly all the time."

"She shack-up with other men?"

"*Hai, takusan* shack-up. She number-one butterfly."

"After she and Bill-san catch house?"

"Before — after — all the time. Yōko black heart, never kind, never love, never passionate, but she love money."

"Bill said she was passionate as hell."

"Imitation," commented Akiko severely.

"You ever make imitation with me?" asked Hank suspiciously.

"Never, Ank-san. Honest and cross heart. First time you touch, my heart like *hibachi* for you."

Hank rose and bowed elaborately. "*Domo arigato gozaimasu.*"

"*Dōitashi mashite.*" Akiko covered her face with her hands.

"Let's go back to the hotel," he said, suddenly eager.

"Please, Ank, not Japanese custom. Everybody *takusan* look. Japanese man never touch *okusan* in daytime."

"The hell they don't! Honest? What's the matter with Japanese men in the daytime?"

"I do not know. Japanese custom is not same. I like

[151]

American custom better. Please, Ank, you not be angry."

"No, never angry, Tangerine. My heart like *hibachi* for you all the time. Why, honey, what's the matter?"

Her face had clouded suddenly and her mouth drooped.

"Please, never speak me Tangerine," she begged. "I hate Tangerine name. I am very sorry have small breasts. I know American man like girl with big breasts, Jane Russell style, I'm sorry."

"Why, Baby-san, that's just a joke. I like your breasts fine. Just right for you. You'd look very funny with Jane Russell breasts. Look here!"

He picked up a reed and drew a sketch in the damp dark sand of a tiny Akiko with Jane Russell breasts, braced a little backward to keep her balance. Akiko laughed until she cried. She picked up the reed and crouched over the sand to draw a tall soldier with his cap pushed back and a cowlick of hair sticking out, like Hank. She looked at it gravely for a minute. Then with a quick stroke she equipped the soldier with a totally improbable endowment, erased the sketch with a stroke of her foot, and hid her face against his shirt. They held each other, laughing like idiots.

"You sure you don't want to go back to the hotel?"

She raised her flushed face from his shirt front and looked behind them toward the pines and ridges.

"I think I like go mountain."

They climbed into the sheltering pines like any pair of honeymooners at a seaside resort. The first day of the flight had begun.

[152   ]

21

IT WAS a funny business, this flight from the long arm of the United States Army. Someway Hank realized he had rather expected one-night camps in hovels and ditchbanks, a quick remove to a new location every few days, sleeping under bridges and up and away before daylight, a perennial transient until his luck ran out. It wasn't that way at all.

They settled down in Omikura like any pair of young newlyweds. Akiko found a house the third day, almost a replica of her house in Nakano before the remodeling. It was amazing how cheaply it could be furnished from the village shops — a pallet and bedding, a few pots and pans, a *hibachi*, and a wooden chest to store clothing in. There was no separate bedroom in the Omikura house and they spread the pallet on the floor of the living room each night.

When the wind was from the sea, it was cool and lovely, with a view from the gallery of the western point and half the harbor. When the wind was off the land, the *benjo* stank almost audibly and Hank would take long walks along the coast or up the river valley. Later he got used to it.

Akiko did the public relations with the community. As she got acquainted with the ladies in the shops she unfolded a brilliant tale of high romance. Her American husband was a soldier who had served out his time in the Army, but when the time came to return to America, he found that he loved her too much to part and so he had elected to remain in Japan. This made the higher American officers very angry and they had threatened to send Army police to find him and take him back to America in a ship. Once in America they would see he was never granted a passport to return. So they had gone to the temple and been married by a Shinto priest because the Army priests had refused the benefits of Christian marriage. Then they had fled to Omikura and she prayed every night the Army would not take him from her to America. She implied that they were both sworn to suicide if the Army had its way.

The story made the rounds of Omikura with the speed of light and they were immediately the object of every kindness. The Japanese are the world's greatest romantics; their literature is studded with hapless lovers who defy tradition and authority to marry out of their station or to live in unwedded bliss. In most stories ruthless parents or police rend them from one another's arms and they commit suicide. Oftentimes the lovers leap from the cliff's edge hand in hand just as the pursuit closes in on them.

Some of the stories are legends and some are history. But it is a fact that double suicides by unhappy lovers became so common that certain spas became famous for their cozy lovers' nests and their conveniently adjacent cliffs. To such towns as the famous resort of Atami the despairing lovers came from all over Japan to revel briefly in bliss and then leap to their death among the rocks and roaring waves a hundred feet below.

Omikura had a reputation for good fishing grounds and fresh vegetables, but it had never been famous as a Lovers' Leap. The Omikurans closed ranks around their first pair of real live runaways. No one was going to drive this gentle pair off the rocks above the rip tide if they could help it. Just the same, they admitted, the Horse's Head rock at the west edge of the narrows was just as appropriate a spot as Atami could boast, especially when the tide was running full to sea.

It was in fact a gay life, charming and delicate, full of leisure and lovemaking, with time for rabbit and pheasant hunting, and picnic dinners on the beach. There was too much time for Hank, used to routine and regular work. He drank the strong Japanese beer in the evenings to put himself to sleep, but each day he rose earlier, before the last stars drowned out in the whitening sky, and walked on the beach, watching the fishing fleet embarking, sometimes helping to draw a seine to the beach before breakfast, and accepting a fresh fish or two from the fishermen.

One day he met Mike Kiuchi. It was midmorning and he was passing the bicycle repair shop on the main street near the hotel when he saw through the open door a young man handling a fine shotgun, handling it in that careful, proud manner of gun lovers, and Hank stepped into the shop. The young Japanese quickly stood the gun behind a bench and turned to him with the rather pained smile with which Hank had learned Japanese greet unwelcome visitors.

"*Ohayo-gozaimasu*," said Hank politely.

"Good morning. I speak English." The man was tall for a Japanese, well built, with two gold-capped incisors, and when he moved, Hank noticed he limped heavily on one leg.

"That's good. I speak very poor Japanese. I hope to learn to speak better soon. I noticed your shotgun. It looks like a very fine piece. I have a double-barreled gun myself, and I thought you might tell me where I could find some good hunting."

The man looked at him soberly for a long time. Then he appeared to make a decision.

"All Omikura knows your story, Sergeant. Is it true you are a deserter?"

"Technically, yes. I must be the first soldier in history that ever deserted to escape a discharge, but it is true."

"Well, then perhaps I can speak to you. I hope you won't tell the Army about my gun collection. You know, of course, Japanese civilians are forbidden to have firearms or ammunition in their possession."

"No, I didn't know that. Why the hell would they care about that?"

"Perhaps they fear we .country people may someday storm the Daiichi Building with birdshot." He smiled pleasantly now, and stuck out his hand. "My name is Mike Kiuchi. We will talk to your pleasure about our guns and about shooting. You like shooting?"

"I like it fine, but I'm a poor shot. For some reason I do best on ducks. Your pheasants are safe. Those downhill crossing shots always fool me."

"The most difficult kind. I think the *kiji* know it here in Japan. In Manchuria, where I hunted before the war one time, it was different. They have much millet there and many pheasants everywhere — fat, stupid birds that run about in easy range. It is almost impossible to make them to fly for the wing shooting."

"Where did you learn such fine English, Mr. Kiuchi?"

"I was a teacher of English at the University of Tokyo. I am a graduate of U.C.L.A. also. Then during the war the teaching of English was discouraged except for intelligence work. I became a pilot. I flew the Betty against your Mustangs, also against Corsairs. It is very difficult to fly the Betty against such aircraft. One acquires great multitudes of holes in his airplane. I think it must have been such a multitude of holes that caused me to cease flying, almost to cease living forever, on Okinawa. My Betty was all right, but very sluggish on the controls, as I came in. At the last minute I leveled off a few feet off the ground. I could not make to go above or below, so I go past the field into the hill. The right leg is now less efficient."

Hank produced cigarettes and they talked — about the war, about guns and hunting, about aircraft, avidly doting on each other's words, their tongues running ahead of

[157]

their thoughts. The bicycles went unmended. Hank hailed an urchin and sent him to the teahouse for cold beer, and they drank.

From time to time a customer dropped into the bicycle shop and Mike would introduce Hank, explain that he was fond of shooting, had a supply of shells. Hank would offer beer and cigarettes and the visitor would join the party. Mike would shout through a side door and the maid from the hotel would bring more beer and clean glasses. Then they would talk some more, with Mike acting as interpreter. By midafternoon Hank and Mike were drunk as owls and there were seven guests in various stages of elevation in the shop. Hank made two trips to the house for cigarettes.

He got back to the house around five o'clock, leaving Mike snoring on a pallet in the rear of the shop, the guests convivially dividing the last bottle, and found Akiko tight-lipped and pale with rage.

"*Takusan* stinko, what a great foolishness!" It was the first time he had ever seen her stamp her foot.

"Wha's matter? Had nice time, met ol' Mike Koochi, good fren', lotsa friend-o. You shut up."

"No, not shut up. One time I speak. You no more drink *takusan bīru*. You not speak all the time to Japanese people. *Takusan bīru, takusan* speak. Pretty soon too much speak. Pretty soon somebody speak C.I.D., you catch police. *Dame desu.*"

"Aw, Baby-san, not ol' Mike. He's good friend-o. Tomorrow I fix the motor in his uncle's boat."

"Tomorrow you shut up, please. Fix boat, O.K. Catch friend, O.K. Drink *takusan, not* O.K. Too much dangerous."

He drank his bowl of tea and collapsed backward, his long legs relaxing slowly across the tiny room until Akiko had to move the table onto the gallery to finish her meal. But in the morning when he wakened he was undressed and in the pallet beside Akiko. His freshly washed khaki coveralls lay folded beside the pallet. Outside, the stars were overcome by a tide of light.

"How did she do it?" he wondered, walking on the wet sand. "How did the little Baby-san get me undressed and into bed, one hundred ninety pounds and all? But then, how does she do many things? How did she pack in ten minutes the night we left Tokyo and still remember to put my coveralls and four cartons of cigarettes in that one suitcase? For that matter, how did she instinctively take mostly Japanese clothes, kimonos and obis, and those white tie-behind smocks for housework? Did she know we'd be living in the country and we'd get on better with the people if she went back to Japanese dress? Or had she planned to run away herself if they shipped me back to the States?

"Come to think of it, how did she know enough to grab that roll of yen and stash it out there with those relatives at Ona? She did that the first day Bill went and told her, as soon as he was gone. I wonder if she's experienced at ducking cops and covering trails. What did that bastard Wentland mean about her being an old Army collaborator from the war? I wonder if she'll ever tell me all of it, and I hope she never does.

"Christ, what a head I've got from that beer bender! I hope Mike and his uncle don't show today."

But they did presently and they went to the ancient motor sampan drawn up on skids on the beach and Hank started working on the one-cylinder two-cycle gas engine. As the sun rose he kept taking out parts and laying them carefully on a clean board while a circle of quiet, respectful fishermen watched him work. Despite the simplicity of the ancient marine motor it was the second day before he found the crack in the hard rubber casing of the ignition coil. He took the coil up to the house and showed Akiko how to dry it, turning it slowly in the smokeless heat of the *hibachi*. After four hours of drying, while he gave the engine a thorough cleaning and scraped the carbon, he located a supply of ordinary rubber bands with Mike's help and jammed them into the crack on the coil casing with a knife blade. Then he melted the rubber with matches until he had a watertight surface. When the rubber dried, he coated the coil with several coats of varnish, and by nightfall of the second day the engine was back together. He shot a generous prime of gasoline into the priming cup of the motor, rocked the heavy flywheel back against compression smartly, and the motor barked briefly and vomited blue smoke.

"Okay," he said to Mike. "Tell Uncle Kajima-san he can launch her now and we'll test her. I think she'll go."

Bystanders pushed the heavy, narrow, knife-prowed craft

into the water. Mike, Hank, and Kajima climbed aboard and Hank started the engine. It ran well, but after a few minutes of listening to the popping engine and watching the exhaust Hank shut her down. He removed the spark plug and narrowed the gap several times, taking a short test run each time and each time shutting down the needle valve on the carburetor a half turn. At last he could detect no roughness in the engine's rhythm, and the exhaust was a faint wisp of pale gray bubbles smoking in their wake.

"Finished," he said, wiping his hands on a bundle of rags. "That's about all I can do. Tell Kajima-san to keep her half throttle or less if he wants these main bearings to last."

They came back to the beach and moored the sampan. Burly Uncle Kajima was profuse in his thanks and Hank matched him gravely, bow for bow. Hank tried to refuse payment, but Mike advised him to take something or Uncle Kajima would lose considerable face and probably be unable to sleep.

"All right, Mike," he said. "Tell him my wife and I are very fond of *tempura*, especially those big prawns and the lobsters you call *ebi*. Ask him to get me a dozen prawns, three lobsters, and a good fresh fish for *tempura*."

So the business was concluded, but Uncle Kajima exceeded his quota of seafood so generously that Hank invited Mike and Mr. and Mrs. Kajima to help them eat *tempura* on Sunday.

The very next day Hank stopped into Mike's shop and helped him repair the coaster brake on a bicycle.

"You like working with motors, do you not, Hank?"

"Sure thing, Mike. Best time I've had in Omikura. It's my trade, you know."

"The repair of Kajima-san's engine was big news here. Bets were laid among the fishermen on the outcome and money changed hands when the engine was restored. I say this because many of the fishermen have engine troubles. There are no new engines for sale in Japan and no money with which to buy them if there were many for sale. What is more serious, there are no parts for many engines. When an engine cannot be fixed, the sampan must go back to sails or sweeps. That means the fisherman must fish closer inshore where the catches are the less. I have another request from a friend who asks you to look at his engine."

"Good enough. I'd like to. Doesn't it run at all?"

"He says it runs well on the very coldest days of winter, but heats so much in the hot weather he cannot make long runs. He is afraid to finish his engine if he runs it so hot. Now in summertime it makes copious steam after five minutes."

"Let's look at it after we get this bike finished. I'll need you for an interpreter, Mike. This sounds easy. If it runs well in winter, it must be getting *some* circulation through the block. If it heats in summer, it isn't getting enough. Probably a leaky pump."

So Hank fixed a second marine engine, and this took only an afternoon. He managed to fabricate a bronze bushing to slow the leak around the worn pump shaft, but still the engine ran too hot after ten minutes. It was the same make as the engine in Kajima-san's sampan, so he readily traced the flow of water through the block. Finally underneath many layers of grease and dirt he found a threaded bronze plug with a setscrew head. The plug entered the water-line fitting at the point where it joined the motor block and was screwed into the line until it was almost closed. Hank backed it out with a screw driver and the engine ran cool enough for him to lay his hand on the cylinder head after a few minutes.

Through Mike he showed the fisherman how to set the plug to lessen the flow for colder weather and increase the engine temperature and how to keep it wide open in summer. The ritual of thanks took a long time again and Hank found out the fisherman's wife kept hens. He arranged for payment in eggs.

Hank became the mechanic of Omikura. He repaired the engines of the fishermen, soldered the water jacket on the charcoal-burning motor bus that ran to Ona, devised a simple self-bailer for another ancient motor sampan that leaked badly, and finally became part owner of a motor sampan.

In the course of fixing engines he met Matsuhashi Hiroshi, a one-armed sergeant, veteran of the China theater. Before Hank had come to Omikura Hiroshi had been the number-one mechanic of the village. Hiroshi had a fine set of tools and knew his business, but like most Japanese mechanics he was content merely to keep an engine running with patchwork and ingenuity. Whether it ran well or poorly did not matter as long as it ran. But he yielded to Hank's ability with no apparent jealousy and became an apt pupil. When he saw the emphasis Hank placed on such details as the spark gap of plugs, timing the flywheel eccentric to get a perfect explosion without the spark's being too early or too late, delicately tuning carburetors for easy starting and efficient combustion, he was quick to learn and follow. Anything Hank did once Hiroshi could do forever after.

Hiroshi owned an ancient sampan, badly dried out, its mast broken, and lacking an engine. But he owned also a vast collection of engine parts, blocks, thrust bearings, universals, shaft logs, water pumps, and odds and ends. In October he asked Hank to help him put together a motor sampan out of assembled engine scraps and the old hull. Together they tackled the problem with the unspeaking concentrated companionship of craftsmen. It was a tough one.

The engine came first. The best and newest block and main motor belonged to an eight-horsepower, two-cylinder, two-cycle Nikura which unfortunately had a crankshaft so far out of round it threw main bearings every twenty to thirty hours of running time. It took ten days to realign the crankshaft and they straightened it by using mostly a flat file and a six-pound sledge. Hiroshi had a micrometer gauge and finally they miked the shaft down to a tolerance almost impossible to measure. They poured babbitt and honed the bearings and set them up tight. They hired a squad of youngsters to turn the shaft by hand until the bearings were seated, six hours of slow-speed revolutions. The rest of the assembly was fairly easy.

Two expert shipwrights restored the hull, calked it, replaced dry-rotted frames and planks, provided a short jury mast which could be stepped in case of engine failure, and helped fit the shaft-log casing into the keel. When it was finished, Hank and Hiroshi took it for a trial run. The engine performed well after a little tuning and it was easily the fastest vessel on Omikura Bay. It leaked a trifle, so although Hiroshi vowed that would cease when the wood swelled the planks, Hank rigged a self-bailer from a piece of pipe to carry the bilge away while running.

They soon discovered a bug, however. The angle of the propeller shaft to the engine was a little too much for their thrust bearing and the bearing ran hot during trials. They could have corrected it by raising the engine bed forward, but Hank was afraid the front main bearing, fed by a splash system, would starve for oil and burn out.

Instead they devised a small jet of cold water running from the pump and playing directly on the thrust plates. The spinning thrust bearing threw a circle of spray over the engine and occupants, but Hiroshi rigged a little wooden spray housing that collected the water and fed it back into the bilge, where Hank's self-bailer carried it away. Now they were in the fishing business, and on fair days they went out on the fishing grounds and hauled the heavy seines by hand. In bad weather they stayed ashore and worked on other fishermen's engines. It was the good time and Hank never wanted it to end.

[165]

2 2

BY OCTOBER they were out of cigarettes, despite self-imposed rationing. Akiko collected all the butts in a can. She dried them, clipped the burned ends, mixed them with Japanese tobacco, and rolled them fresh each day. She gave up smoking, except for rare occasions when they had guests for a meal, and held Hank down to four cigarettes a day. They had no sugar, and salt was hard to get. Hank was short of clothes. Besides the set of summer-weight OD's he had worn the night they fled he had brought four extra shirts, six changes of underwear, and three pairs of socks in the musette bag. Akiko had brought his coveralls from the house in Nakano. He hated to wear a shirt and trousers while repairing engines and fishing, because they were his best clothes, and it took a long time and much soap to wash them. They had been out of American soap for months. Akiko shopped for rough cloth in the village and helped a seamstress make him four pairs of coveralls like his OD's.

Now they spoke mostly in Japanese, for his language

ability had multiplied in Omikura. Akiko, with little chance to use English except occasionally with Hank or Mike, abandoned her sporadic attempts to master the difficult foreign words. One night she said, "Tomorrow I will take the bus to Ona and meet my second sister, Sumiko. She is bringing me things we need from Tokyo."

"How does she know where you are?"

"She does not know exactly. My relatives in Ona have told her that things which are mine can be brought to their house. I have sent Mrs. Osato twice and Mrs. Nakamura once with messages on the motor bus. They leave them at my cousin's house and go away."

"Suppose Sumiko asks that taxi driver where he left us?"

"He can talk only through his mother. He is a voiceless one, poor fellow. Yes, he will say, perhaps, that he took us to Omikura, but he believes it was our purpose to take a fishing boat for the island of Oshima as soon as we came. I am sorry to have so little intelligence in this important matter, but, you remember, the haste was great and a woman is always foolish when she is in haste. If I had had more time to plan, I would have told a better lie."

"You are my number-one favorite liar, little one. I could not have done half as well. From this day you shall tell all my lies for me. Will there be cigarettes and sugar perhaps?"

"Not from Sumiko. She has no way to get these things. But Ona is on the railroad going north and so we can buy a little sugar and American cigarettes from the black market. There is a black market wherever the railroad goes from

Tokyo. I must get also some army blankets of woolen for the winter and to make a winter coat for you. We must be careful of the money. It is enough for living in the country, but it goes fast when buying things from the black market."

"Won't it be dangerous for you? The Tokyo police may have given your description to the Ona police. It will be a great weight on my heart while you are gone. Return swiftly and make my heart light again."

"I will be most careful and come back the same day. My heart is too heavy away from you. Do not worry for me, please. If I do well and bring things we need and that please you, it will be a happy time."

"All things you do are well done and please me very much. You keep our house clean and wash the clothes. You prepare cooked meals American style with eggs for breakfast and it is double work to feed an American and takes much time and charcoal. You sing me sweet songs and wash my back when I am tired and sore."

Hank gathered her in his arms and kissed her. And looking in her eyes as the kiss went on and on, he saw how she had changed. For the old agate-hard glitter never shrouded her eyes any more. There had been something reptilian in her passion before. Now her eyes stayed deep and soft, deeper and softer than ordinarily, and still their bodies came to each other every time as hungrily as ever. He released her gently.

"There is a thing also you do better than all others and that pleases me more than all else. Let us do this thing now."

"It is the night for us to go to the *ofuro* and I must be ready for the bus journey tomorrow. May we not go first to the *ofuro* and bathe, and then we will come here and do this thing that pleases you and me?"

"I have a better idea. Let us do first the so pleasant thing I speak of, and then let us go next to the *ofuro* for the baths, and let us come here quickly from the *ofuro* and do again what pleases ourselves."

"Damn tootin'," laughed Akiko, hurling herself at his chest.

Lying awake that night on the pallet, with her head on his shoulder and her hair, fragrant from the bath, scenting the sharp October night smell, they talked as they had so many nights before.

"Are you sad for your country and your people, Ank-san? I have brought you great trouble, and now you must live like a bandit in a poor Japanese village. It is my fault for wanting all that money. I am a bad woman."

"Do not speak so. I am happy here with you. Perhaps I may be sad for my own country on certain days when I think of it. But it is not often and I forget it quickly when I hold you in my arms. I forbid you to call yourself bad woman."

"You are too kind. Is it different for American men? Japanese men would not want a woman who had been touched. I have done many bad things, some things I can never speak of for shame. But the thing I did for you was bad. I wish I had never spoken with Chang. All my life I have been crazy for money. It is a sickness and I cannot help it. And also I wish I was your Only the first time in Shinjuku. I wish you were the first man to touch me. Would that have pleased you?"

"Yes, I think it would now. But when we first met, it was different. My flesh was thirsty for you, but my heart was cold. Now my body is happy next to yours and my heart is happy against your heart."

"It is very strange. I am so ignorant, being a Japanese. If I had a Japanese husband, we would never talk like this. We would not speak of love or lovemaking as you and I do in the night. Perhaps a young man might speak of love to a beautiful geisha or an entertainer he wished to sleep with, but not to his wife. But I am happy to speak with you as we do. I will be your loving geisha, your *koibito*, and your wife."

"I love you," he whispered in English, lips close to her ear and his face buried in the cloud of soap-scented hair.

"I love you," she said in Japanese, and they turned together, straining close with clutching hands.

George Yamamoto kept working. He didn't have to — the case was finished. Nothing to do but find Mueller and run him through a court. But unofficially, very unofficially, but very certainly, George was unsatisfied. He dropped in on Bill Zarnowski at the Motor Pool Command one day and talked briefly.

"Not a word — not a sign since the night he left," Zarnowski assured him. "Not the girl, either. Do you suppose they could be dead?"

"Could be," said George. "But why should they be? No motive."

"Suppose they had a large sum of money. People have been killed for money, I've heard."

"How large a sum?"

"Several thou — Or any amount at all — just so it was enough to interest a potential killer."

"What makes you think he'd have any money at all?"

"Well" — Zarnowski smiled a little self-consciously — "you guys want him for something, right? Most of your investigations involve money, I always thought, black marketeering and so on, right? And he lived well, car, fancy clothes for his girl, a house of their own, right? It just figures that way — to me."

"You have a car, a better one than Mueller had. You have a better house, and a girl with more clothes. You expect to be murdered for your money — or accused of black-marketing?"

"I thought you were looking for information about Mueller."

"I am. Good-by, Lieutenant. Let me know if you hear anything."

George went away from the motor pool, thinking. "He can't make up his mind. He wants us suspicious of Mueller, but he doesn't want him caught, and he's not altogether loyal to Mueller, that's a cinch. Someone in that family knows where the girl is, and that's where Mueller is. No use talking to that bitchy beauty Yōko again. She's a better liar than Zarnowski — much better. I might as well quit asking and start looking — when I have the time."

So he kept looking — mostly at the comings and goings around the Watanabe household in Shinjuku. Nothing happened — no suspicious visits, no suspicious trips. Once on a school holiday the pudgy little sister Sumiko make a trip to Ona in Chiba Prefecture. George checked her destination just after she bought a ticket in Asakusa, but he was in uniform and decided it wasn't worth following her — not that day. Someday he'd take a trip to Ona — especially if Little Sister made other trips.

23

Akiko left early on the bus for Ona, and Hank helped Hiroshi haul the seine for sardines in the bay. He never worried when he was busy. Between them they had rigged a power take-off windlass on the foredeck of the sampan and let the motor haul the lines after the net was laid. When the bag was completed, they took the end which was fast at the stern and dragged it forward to close the bag. If the catch was worth lifting, they scooped as much as a bushel of the tiny fish, actually no bigger than minnows, into the baskets. Many times they moved the craft and laid the net in a different spot because the catch was too light to bother lifting. What made the day interesting were the occasional schools of mackerel running in the bay. When there was a fair catch of sardines, many of the smallest ones wriggled through the meshes of the seine when they were being bagged. The mackerel lay just outside the belly of the seine and fed on the emerging minnows in swift rushes, their silver flanks gleaming swiftly in the sun as they struck at the bait fish.

Hiroshi showed Hank how to catch the mackerel by jigging a little gauzy-winged fly on a stiff bamboo pole just outside the net. The mackerel were worth more than the sardines and by midafternoon they had thirty-three of the bigger fish and five baskets of sardines.

Hank knocked off seining at three o'clock and went to the bus stop by the hotel. He talked for twenty minutes with Mike in the bicycle shop and then the bus was coming down the street. A block away he recognized her pageboy bob. She was already standing by the door of the bus, and his heart turned over. It was the first time he had known the extent of his fear for Akiko.

When all the boxes and bundles had been carried up to the house on the hill, they talked over a precious brew of coffee sweetened with real sugar.

"I am sorry about the black-market things," said Akiko. "Everything is now too expensive for us to have many cigarettes, or coffee, or sugar. I bought only a little. You would never believe the prices they charge. It is because of the new rate of the yen which the Americans have made."

"What's that? Did they change the rate again?"

"Yes, a big change this time. When you came to Japan, the yen was fifteen for one dollar. Then in a few months it was thirty-six. That was when we sold the money to Chang. Now it is seventy-two for one dollar. We have the same amount of yen with which we came to Omikura but only half as many dollars. Everything on the black market is doubled. I did not take enough money for all the things we need for winter. I must go again for the army blankets and one of those heavy blue navy coats for you."

"Did you see the little sister and is there still trouble with the police? Tell me everything."

"Well, then, let us smoke one cigarette and I will tell you. Sumiko was already at the house of my cousin when I came on the bus. She came on the early train. You remember Sumiko, who is fifteen by American methods of telling a girl's age? She is not my double sister but only single."

"You mean half sister, same as Yōko and the others."

"Not the same." Akiko smiled quickly and kept her eyes down. "First I was born before my father married and I lived with my mother for four years or perhaps as many as six. I think it must have been six, because I remember a little. She was very beautiful and had many admirers and was always going to parties, but I was always left with an ugly old woman. I remember my mother would sometimes sing while she fixed her hair and she had a fine voice. I would have loved her very much, I think.

"But then my father married in the temple, and before the first year of his marriage ended, he came and brought me to my new mother. I sometimes think he was paying money to my real mother and this way was less expensive for him. Then my brothers and sisters were born in Nakano, where we lived, all but Sumiko."

"He got another girl pregnant?"

"Yes, that is how it was. Sumiko's mother was a young girl from the country, with poor manners and little education. My father brought Sumiko home also when she was a

[175]

baby. My mother and Sumiko I love more than all my people. Sumiko is the one I trust above everyone. She tells always the truth to me and never repeats a secret. My mother is always kind and loves all her children well. I have made her heart heavy many times and still she loves me. My father I hate."

"I only saw your third sister twice. She does not look like the others or like you."

"Yes, she is a very plain girl, but has a good heart. Well, then, my third sister was waiting at my cousin's house and told me many things. In Tokyo the police come to my mother's house every week and they have questioned all my brothers and sisters. For a time they thought you were hiding there and the American police came with them twice, but she thinks the police believe my family does not know where we are now. It is true. Before today, no one knew where we had gone. Now only Sumiko knows that we are somewhere not far from Ona, and she will never tell, not even my brothers and sisters.

"The police searched the house in Nakano many times, but at last they let my family rent it to a Japanese family, and my father takes the rent money. My mother, however, makes him give her part of the money, which she saves for me. I told Sumiko to tell my mother to use the money for herself. It would not keep us long when our money is gone, anyway.

"The Americans took your jeep from the motor pool and have it locked up inside a wire fence on A Avenue downtown. Lieutenant Bill-san was also questioned, but only once, Yōko told her. The lieutenant has said he would help us if he could, but I do not trust Yōko. Bill-san told Yōko and Sumiko if they hear from me to say, 'Let him know if you need anything.' "

"Don't worry about Bill and Yōko," said Hank, breaking into English. "I think they never speak anything. They like better we stay in country, police never catch. Maybe if police catch me, they worry C.I.D., find out they sell greenback money, too."

Akiko thought this over. Then she nodded soberly. "I think true. If we need something too much, we speak Lieutenant Zarnowski. Other things Sumiko catch.

"Well, then," she went on in Japanese again, "there is not much more of the news Third Sister brings. She thinks Yōko and Bill-san have much trouble and many quarrels. Yōko does not wish to stay in the house all day and wants to go dancing every night. Also she will not cook meals, but hires a woman to cook and clean. Sumiko says Yōko has much money hidden away which Bill-san has given her."

Hank did not reply, but drew up his knees and stared at the wall. After a quick look at his face Akiko rose and began preparing the evening meal. She had grown used to his sudden moods of preoccupation, although in the beginning she had feared them. When he grew silent and thoughtful, Akiko would fear that he was grieving for America, for his Army friends, regretting his life with her that had made him a hunted man living like a peasant in a poor Japanese coastal village. But as time passed, she

[177]

learned that his periods of quiet study usually concerned some problem of their existence together, and when he had studied it out, he would talk to her about it.

But Hank was worried this time and thinking didn't help. He wished he had studied more about economics, how inflation worked, what made money sound and what made it worthless. He thought he knew what made Japanese money worth anything at all and that was American dollars. If the Americans pegged the yen at five hundred to one, that made the yen worth a fifth of a cent no matter what. He knew inflation, especially in defeated nations following a long war, went in a climbing spiral. The rate of exchange had been changed twice since he had come to Japan and each time it had resulted in devaluation of the yen by one hundred per cent.

At first the new cheaper yen seemed to buy as much as ever in ordinary Japanese goods. But on the black market American goods immediately cost twice as much, then in a few days the rest of the prices followed suit, and eventually rice, fish, meat, and vegetables would cost just twice as much. They had a stake of approximately seventy-five hundred dollars in yen when they fled to Omikura. Now it was worth three thousand seven hundred fifty dollars. Living as they did, they didn't spend five hundred dollars a year, but if the spiral went on, their savings would be cut every time the yen was pegged at a new devalued ratio. As fugitives, they needed a bankroll for emergencies. He didn't know what "emergencies" to expect, but he knew they would come.

Even after the meal was finished and they had walked to the *ofuro* for their baths and returned, he was still silent. And when they were close together on the narrow pallet, she felt the silence and the fear as their lips met in darkness. Her hand crept gently around his shoulder; tiny fingers whispered like silk up and down the little vertebral hills and valleys. She could not walk with him where his strange foreign thoughts traveled, but she could exorcize the regrets of the past and the fears of the future by claiming him for the present.

And Akiko knew there was no present in all the world beyond this, as she felt his body answer and his arms engulf her. There was only the great Now that filled them, the racing blood currents through the flesh, the hearts that soared like kites on a great wind. And, later, exhaustion, that was a part of the warm, friendly darkness, and sleep, coming slow and sure.

She whispered to him. "Don't worry, Ank-san. We be O.K."

24

BEGINNING in late October Hank and Mike Kiuchi started hunting. For the most part they hunted only in the early morning and late afternoon, bicycling out of Omikura into the hilly Chiba countryside with their shotguns broken down and lashed to the crossbars. Hank was surprised at the variety of game. The thickets in the ravines and on the steep slopes and hilltops held pheasant, giant hares, and bamboo grouse that held close and only flushed from under his feet. Ducks were coming down from Siberia to winter along the coast, and they frequently got jump shooting for teal and widgeon along the river. In the evening they often waited under the giant water elms along the river where droppings indicated a dove roost. These were the wild *hato*, considered a great delicacy.

Ammunition was hard to come by. Hank had three and a half boxes of shells, which he shared with Mike. He quickly learned to leave the wing shots to Mike in order to save shells. Mike was virtually infallible at medium range. But in the main Hank became an expert sneak hunter and pot shooter. He learned to crawl on his belly after a pheasant or grouse, make careful shots to concentrate the pattern in the head or neck and save the meat. Along the river he learned patience as he waited among the willows for sitting ducks to move into range. When his shells were all gone, they used hand-loaded shells prepared by Mike, a low-velocity load of unreliable pattern, but they improved their chances by stalking their game even closer than before.

The big hares looked like an oversize cottontail rabbit, weighing seven or eight pounds each, and were fairly easy game as they usually flushed from low cover near cultivated fields and often ran straightaway across the bare cultivated earth. As the autumn moved into winter, the flocks of ducks along the coast multiplied into great rafts of birds over the tide flats with smaller flocks moving up the river at dawn and sunset to forage briefly in fresh water. Mike learned that the bluebill and widgeon tended to be fishy and tough, since they fed heavily on seaweed and shellfish. Teal were dumb and easily shot but were too small to waste shells on. Best of all was a duck he had never before seen. The Japanese name meant "long-feathered" and the drakes were fawn-colored with iridescent green necks. On the trailing edge of each wing were long outward-curving primary feathers that whistled shrilly in flight. The ducks were wary but could be decoyed with Mike's blocks on stormy days of high winds and driving rain.

Hank and Mike moved slowly through the Chiba hills. They made frequent rest stops, for Mike's stiff leg could not stand more than five or six minutes of steady hiking on rough ground. Many times as they rested, chatting, they flushed game almost at their feet. Hank marveled at the abundance of wildlife in a country so densely populated and where food, especially meat, was so scarce and expensive.

"It was the war," said Mike. "Before the war there was little game except on the shooting preserves of wealthy men. The winter duck flight was not one third of what it is now. But during the war, even before Pearl Harbor when we were fighting only in China, all guns and ammunition were confiscated for scrap and for the Army. Then you Americans came and made it unlawful to own arms and ammunition. The game got a chance and is coming back fast in the countryside."

"Then, the country people, the farmers, don't ever get any game?"

"Oh, yes, with traps and snares, but not much. They set hooks baited with corn for ducks along the watercourses and catch some that way. But they do not catch many birds or rabbits. Mostly they are too busy with agriculture."

"I notice the farmers are very friendly. They leave their fields to show us where they have seen pheasants and doves, and always wish us good hunting. Have the country people always been like this?"

"No, as a rule they are shy and do not talk to strangers. It is because you are an American they are so friendly. You see, under the occupation we are getting land reform and this is the first year many of these people own their own farms. Naturally they credit the Americans for making them landowners instead of tenants. You would be less popular with the big landlords from whom the land is taken."

"They don't have to pay for the land, then?"

"Oh, yes. They pay a very low valuation and a very low rate of interest. Most of the loans run for thirty years. Little by little the landlords will get a part of the value of their farms back. They should, perhaps, feel lucky to get anything. Certainly the Americans under General MacArthur could have taken the land away without paying them anything. But the Japanese middle class and aristocracy do not like slow pay in small amounts. They would like to keep the tenant system as a hedge against inflation. Also they would prefer lump sums of cash, so they could quickly form new business ventures. The Japanese businessman is the true capitalist of the Orient. He believes in *laissez faire*."

Hank stood, scuffing his right foot lightly against the pebbled wash of the ravine lip, his gunstock resting on the other toe. The mention of inflation bothered him.

"This inflation of the yen, Mike — do you think it will keep getting worse?"

"Yes, unfortunately. I think it will form the same pattern as all postwar currency inflations in history. It will get worse until the economy of Japan reaches stability. Then it will level off. Someday, after many years, it may regain its old value."

Mike paused and looked at Hank a rather long time, and then he went on.

"It is a poor time for Japanese to have savings in the form of cash. They can be halved at a stroke down at GHQ. It is better to have the money invested in land or durable goods that will outlast this reconstruction period. Fortunately I have no savings, only my books, my guns, and my bicycle shop. When I sell a bicycle, I buy another, so that I do not accumulate money."

"Yes," said Hank thoughtfully. "I see what you mean."

"But it's one thing to understand, Hank, old shack rat," he told himself as they walked on, "and it's a problem for sergeants — what the hell you're gonna do about it. You can't invest your little pile of yen in a shop or business unless it's one you could carry in a musette bag. You gotta be ready to take it on the hop when the whistle blows. All you can do is hold on to your lousy roll while it melts in your pocket. Then you can turn yourself in or else come up with a smart answer."

"Do you think I could get a job if I go broke?" he asked.

"Certainly. You have a job now. You are the mechanic of marine engines for Omikura, and you have the fishing boat to work with Hiroshi. Neither pays much by American standards, but it is something. You are foolish not to take money for your work and it shames the people you work for that you ask only for a fresh fish or some eggs as a token payment."

"I would not know what to ask. What would be fair wages for a mechanic?"

"I should say twenty-four yen an hour. That's a third of a dollar at the present rate, but about right for skilled labor. The fish business, of course, depends on the market and the luck."

"There goes one!" shouted Hank, but the blast of Mike's gun covered his words and a hurtling bamboo grouse cartwheeled in the air and slumped into a tangle of vines on the opposite slope of the ravine. Hank retrieved the bird and handed it to Mike and they returned toward where they had left the bicycles.

"Starting tomorrow, Mike," said Hank, "I'm a twenty-four-yen-an-hour man. The wolf is not yet at the door, but I can hear his howls getting plainer."

"I am familiar with this idiom," said Mike. "If the noise of this wolf becomes very intense, please come to me as a friend and perhaps we can think of proper actions."

George Yamamoto, now First Lieutenant Yamamoto, came to Ona on business — nothing to do with the long-missing Sergeant Henry Mueller. George had come as close to forgetting about Akiko and Hank as he could, but the very name of the town kept nagging him as he prowled the alleys in his plain clothes. There was a thriving black market in food and army goods functioning almost openly in a street of stalls near the railroad station. George looked the stalls over, ignoring the ones that offered only a few Hershey bars and Lucky Strikes, but he gave more attention to the ones that sold army blankets, combat boots, bulk sugar, and penicillin. At these he made purchases for evidence and noted the ones which accepted occupation scrip as willingly as yen. Those were the operators that had an illegal currency traffic and a source of contraband leading inside the Army. The others were simply commission retailers.

And then he saw the girl buying an army blanket at a stall and he remembered what he had forgotten about the town.

The impact left him in shock. He was unable to understand the wild feeling that lifted his heart and dropped it — a crazy mixture of fear, discovery, and pity. He had never felt it before, and it bewildered him now. He should feel satisfaction and the keen excitement of the chase. Two years now and it all dropped in his lap. Ona was where the homely sister went. Ona was where the missing Akiko Watanabe was, right here in front of him. And Ona was the hideout of Sergeant Mueller, if he was still alive. All he had to do was follow the girl.

Why, then, did he feel sorrow, as though something piteous and miserable had happened to himself? He followed her automatically as she walked quickly through the streets, but his feet were heavy. He carried a pocketful of minutes — her minutes, her very last ones — and with each step she threw one away. All this time they had been here — had they been happy together? Faithful to each other? Quarrelsome, discontented, nagged by regret? Another few steps — a trickle of seconds — and he would know and they would be destroyed.

Akiko went straight to the little bus station, a half block

from the railroad office. George took up his watch across the street in a noodle shop and ordered a bowl of noodle soup. It was a raw day, but the fragrant steaming soup had no appeal. He sniffed it, tasted it, put down his spoon, and watched.

She was waiting for a bus. So there were more minutes to dribble along the way. A bus ride to another town — or waiting for Mueller to join her. Maybe he was coming in on a bus to rendezvous with her. Or was the girl waiting for a third person — a courier from Tokyo, a relative or friend bringing money and food — that stolid younger sister with the thick legs?

How on earth had they managed so long? He tried to remember the old file in the office. How much was it? Maybe five or six thousand in yen. But the rate of exchange would have cut that to a quarter by now. The girl was neatly dressed in a simple kimono and wooden geta, no more tailored suits and snakeskin pumps with matching accessories. But she looked healthy, still the same old-child face, calm and wearing a tiny, musing half smile, a little girl hugging a delicious secret.

Too bad for them — for himself, too. They weren't even important now — not compared to some of his cases. The field grader with the gold welded under the fenders of his car they had picked up last month at the port of embarkation in Yokohama — or the GHQ finance officer they hadn't picked up yet, but would just as soon as he ran another half a million through the black market and pocketed the difference between the official and black-market rate of exchange. These days they weren't bothering with fellows like Mueller and his girl — except for that blue-seal currency business — that did make it bad.

Impulsively he dropped the spoon and laid some yen on the table and walked out of the noodle shop. He went straight across the street to the bus station and stood before her.

He had seen them before like this — trapped and desperate, shrunken with fear — but not like this, either — eyes filmed with shock and despair, dying almost visibly under his eyes. He felt a sudden necessity to be kind, to get it over with quickly, to end her suffering — so like a crippled animal.

"Watanabe-san," he said formally, "come outside. We must talk."

He took her arm and the largest of her packages and felt her totter with faintness in the doorway, but her step strengthened as they crossed the street. In the clattering steps of her wooden clogs he could sense the return of courage; now she would fight, lie, stall, or try to escape. They were all the same.

They walked into the almost deserted waiting room of the railroad station and sat on the hard benches.

"Tell me where he is," he said. "Where is Sergeant Mueller?"

"I don't know." Her voice was low and even.

"It is useless to lie, Watanabe-san. I can go to the bus station and check your ticket — where you came from. Then I go to this town and wait in the bus station. Pretty soon he is worried because you do not return and he comes to the bus station. It is easy. You had better tell me."

"He is not waiting for me any longer. He is gone far away."

George, from long experience, sensed that she had developed a hasty lie and now would stick to it desperately. "Then why are you here and not at home?"

"I am afraid of the Tokyo police. They beat me before."

"You should have told me. I would have seen that you were treated fairly. It is not permitted to beat persons under interrogation — it is an occupation regulation."

She was mute and he waited. The station was filling up with people buying tickets and queuing up on the platform beside the tracks.

He repeated gently, "Why not tell me? One way or the other, it makes little difference."

"I told you. He is gone."

"Where — when did he go?"

"I do not know where. Back to the United States, maybe. Over a year ago. I have heard nothing since. He said he would hide on a ship leaving Japan."

"All this is no good, foolish girl. I can find out easily. You should tell me the truth. After all, it is not a lifetime at stake. He has broken the law and must be punished — by imprisonment, a few years maybe. It is not worth all this trouble and lies. It is not forever."

He heard the moan of the approaching train and felt the station floor begin to shake with the beat of the drive wheels. On the platform passengers settled their armloads

[189]

of bundles, and mothers tightened their grips on children. Akiko shook her head and looked out the door.

"I told you," she said. "He is gone."

He followed her gaze out to the platform, sensing some purpose in her widening eyes and stiffening features. Her running figure flashed before him, streaking for the platform. She ran quietly in her sock feet, having kicked off her clogs. He gave a great leap, almost caught her in the door, lost a step as her smaller figure threaded the passenger queue while he bumped clumsily, and saw her purpose as she swung alongside the moving train and inclined in a sidelong dive toward the clattering trucks of the coaches. She broke her stride quickly as a man's form standing at the very edge of the platform barred her way, managed to stop, and then bent her head and leaned into the wheels.

George knew in a blazing microinstant of clarity that he was going too fast. The only way to reach her was to go into the train, and in the same light-fast process, faster than thought, he knew that he would and must. He caught her arm above the elbow, yanked her like a weightless doll up and away, and rolled his shoulder to the side of the moving coach as he overran the platform. He felt the shoulder strike the coach, his body roll with the train's slowing motion, knew one foot was still on the platform but that he was too far to come back, rolling with his back to the coach now and straining to return to the utterly impossible balance on his feet, when he felt the hard blow on his back.

He never knew what it was for sure — the handrail perhaps, at the rear entrance to the coach — but the sudden breath-robbing crash against his side and back threw him violently out and forward, stumbling across the platform where women screamed and men scurried and shouted.

Akiko lay at his feet, her kimono hiked up to her buttocks. He picked her up and pushed through the crowd into the station. He propped her on a bench and whipped around to the pale dispatcher and showed his badge. His voice snapped.

"Tell the police there is to be no investigation. This is United States Army business. I will take charge, you understand?"

The dispatcher almost nodded his head off. Then he bowed deeply for good measure. When he straightened up, George had gone out of the station, carrying the girl.

He put her in a waiting taxi, feeling her come to life, one tiny arm making clutching motions at the empty air on the side away from him. "Take the road to Chiba," he told the driver and looked out the rear window for a glimpse of a frozen throng of people staring from the platform.

When he turned to her, she was conscious, sitting up in the corner of the seat, the tears beginning to slide down her cheekbones, but tranquil and not making any noise. "How like our Japanese women," he thought, watching her. "Even when they weep, they make it a small, delicate thing." And then he scowled, for it was the first time he could remember that he had thought of the Japanese as "our" women or "our" anything. It was always *them*. Why should he feel suddenly this identification with a miserable Tokyo street girl, he, George Yamamoto, a third-generation Hawaiian, with nothing in common but a facility in their language?

"It was an accident," he said. "I was not looking for you or for him. I came to Ona about another matter and happened to see you on the street."

"It doesn't matter now," she said. "At first I thought it would happen the next day, or the next week, but I knew it would happen sometime."

"Is he well?"

"He is thinner but well enough. I wish it had not been me that you saw. I do not want to bring the police to him. In a little while he would have come back of his own will."

"Why do you say that?"

"He speaks of it in his sleep and I know it is always in his thoughts. I know him well now, and anyway, a woman knows these things."

"I have to do something about this," he said most angrily. "That business at the railroad station will be reported. You understand it cannot be helped?"

"I understand," she said and gave the quick headshake that flipped the fat tears from her cheekbones.

"It was very foolish what you did. This is not a matter for suicide. He will live many years. Do you wish him to remember you crushed under the wheels of a train? He would blame himself all his life."

"It was foolish," she agreed. "I did not want to live,

knowing that I had been the cause of his trouble and then led the police to him. It is too much."

"Listen, girl," George said. "There is a chance I can help you a little. Only a chance, understand — and only for a little while. You think he will give himself up before long?"

"I do not know when. He will do it in time. There is no doubt."

"I must make a report to my office. In another mile we will pass the Chiba Ordnance Depot and I can use the Army telegraph. Will you wait with the taxi driver and not run away? I may be gone for more than an hour."

"I will wait."

George made his way to the Communication Center and struggled with the TX message form.

HAVE CUSTODY OF AKIKO WATANABE WANTED FOR QUES-
TIONING IN CASE OF SERGEANT HENRY MUELLER X MUELLER
DISAPPEARED WHILE BEING QUESTIONED RE ILLEGAL YEN
SALES IN 1948 X SUSPECT GIRL KNOWS

George stopped and bit his pencil and frowned out the window over the bank of clattering teletypes. Technically he didn't have custody — not just now — and he couldn't project his suspicions of what Akiko might or might not know. He crumpled the blank and put it in his pocket and began again.

BELIEVE GIRL SEEN IN ONA MAY BE A WATANABE INVOLVED
1948

[193]

He crumpled that one and the next and the next. Finally he completed his draft and filed it with the landline operator to encode.

INTERRUPTED ONA MISSION TO CHECK ON GIRL SEEN ON STREET X SOMEWHAT RESEMBLES JAPANESE GIRL UNDER INVESTIGATION FOR ILLEGAL YEN SALES 1948 X REFER FILE ON SERGEANT HENRY MUELLER X CASE UNCLOSED X REQUEST INSTRUCTIONS X

He waited, smoking, in the Communication office, remembering that Reilly would be O.D. now, and Reilly was lazy and given to wisecracks. He hadn't really lied to them — he had never lied. He wasn't supposed to leave an important job without instructions. That was Standard Operating Procedure. It was up to them. He'd do what they said.

Half an hour went by and the sergeant on watch beckoned him to the grilled window and handed him the decoded reply.

SUGGEST CONCENTRATE ON ORIGINAL ASSIGNMENT X CHASE STREET GIRLS ON YOUR OWN TIME X REILLY X

George grinned and put the message carefully in his wallet. He might need it someday. He went back to the taxi, waiting up the street from the entrance to the military reservation, with a light step. It was a fine feeling to bring this kind of news. On the way back to Ona he told her.

"As I remember, you never admitted your name was

Akiko Watanabe. I may have been mistaken. If I see Sergeant Mueller, I shall arrest him, but my office has ordered me to investigate another matter. If you see Mueller-san, you may tell him what happened today or not. Please yourself."

She looked at him, trying to understand, then cried, "You are too kind. You will have trouble because of this. It is bad luck to be kind to me — my luck is all bad."

"Perhaps it will improve, now," he said.

They rode in silence until they were on the edge of Ona once more. He left the taxi three blocks from the bus depot and paid the driver. As he got out, she said, "I can never tell him. It would burden him too much. My thanks are all I can give you and they are worthless."

"Stay away from trains," he said, "and away from Ona."

25

MIKE was the only man in Omikura who had a library of books in English. During the winter of 1948-1949 Hank read every word of every book Mike owned. He read *The Flowering of New England*, three volumes of A. E. Housman's poems, a volume of Walt Whitman, and three books of arctic and antarctic exploration by Richard E. Byrd. He read for the second time *Moby Dick*, *Return of the Native*, and *Wintersmoon*. He found two books by Beebe on his prewar investigations of marine depths and a stack of literary magazines from the thirties. Best among these was a magazine devoted exclusively to short stories by promising young writers, called *Story*, and Hank read it avidly.

He hunted with Mike and he fished almost daily, weather permitting, with Hiroshi, usually called Gunso, or Sergeant, in recognition of his Army service. By midwinter Hank was on visiting terms with a dozen commercial fishermen, the veterinarian who practiced among the paddy farmers in the Chiba back country, the dentist, Dr. Yamaguchi, Mrs.

Omachi, the midwife, and the Omikura chief of police, a retired Imperial Army noncom, Tabata Goro. Chief Tabata was a portly man of vast dignity who wore his title without dispute since he was the only law-enforcement man in Omikura. On rare occasions he hunted with Hank and Mike, using an ancient single-hammer gun with a stub twist barrel. In a town as small as Omikura the chief was undoubtedly aware that Hank was more or less a fugitive, but he carefully refrained from embarrassing inquiries. Hank got the idea that the chief wasn't going to bother him unless someone else forced his hand.

He was twenty pounds under his normal weight now. Akiko kept taking in the waistline of his trousers and worrying about the way his ribs showed when they went to the *ofuro*. And despite the fact that they probably lived better and ate more than ninety-five per cent of the Omikurans, he was always hungry. Since leaving Tokyo, he had not seen or tasted an orange or lemon. Milk or cheese was unknown. Sugar and chocolate came only rarely and in small amounts from Akiko's infrequent trips to the Ona black market. There were plenty of fresh vegetables, tangerines, and wonderful apples in season, potatoes, rice, fish, seafood, and a little expensive beef and pork to be had. On rare occasions they bought a chicken and had a feast. Most of their bakery goods had to be bought, such as bread, jelly rolls filled with sweetened bean curd, and noodles. Akiko had never learned to bake.

The game he brought in from hunting trips was a welcome change of diet, but except in the coldest weather was likely to spoil before it was consumed. There was no refrigeration, no ice, and no cold storage in Omikura. When the fishermen brought in heavy catches of sardines and king mackerel, the fish buyers from the neighboring port of Sintobashi only had to wait a few hours to beat the price down. Unless quickly sold and transported, the fish would spoil and they brought considerably less as dried, salted, or pickled fish.

On Thanksgiving Day, Hank helped Akiko bake a large black mutant pheasant cock that he had shot. It was quite a trick to bake anything on a *hibachi*, but Hank made an oven from a tin box, and after six hours of slow baking the bird was done to a turn. All stuffed with apples, nuts, and bread crumbs, it made a fine meal. Akiko pronounced it delicious and ate heartily, but was appalled at the expense, due to the amount of charcoal consumed.

Probably it was expense more than anything, Hank decided, that made most Japanese eat fish and seafood raw or lightly salted in brine. Most of the time he got along very well, dipping his bits of fish fillets in a mixture of oil and tangerine juice, but he dreamed of lemons and roast beef.

Tempura was a fine Japanese dish, or, rather, a ceremonial meal. It consisted principally of heavily breaded prawns, lobster tails, oysters, and fresh fish deep-fried in oil. It was reserved for special occasions, such as New Year's. And the New Year was more than a day to the Japanese. It was a whole holiday season beginning January 1 and running for three consecutive days. It was a time for dressing up in their best blue kimonos for the men and their brightest red kimonos for the women. No one in all Omikura seemed too poor to have one fine kimono for the New Year feast. For three days no one worked. Sedate men and women played a game like badminton, with flat paddles and a feathered puck, in the streets. In the evenings some of the men gathered around a drinking table in the town's hotel and sang songs and drank themselves into insensibility or violence. The tolerance of the average Japanese for alcohol seemed amazingly low to Hank. They got drunk quickly and easily, probably due somewhat to their diet, and passed quickly through the customary stages of drunks everywhere.

First they became fraternally affectionate. They loved to repeat the American ritual of handshaking endlessly with Hank. They swore eternal friendship and blood brotherhood with tears in their eyes. But in a few minutes they passed to quarreling or snoring. It cost little for a Japanese to get drunk, Hank decided.

The best New Year's custom of all was the payment of debts. Every fisherman and motor owner in Omikura who owed Hank money for repair work came punctiliously on New Year's morning or the following morning to pay his bill. Akiko did the honors by serving tea, hot wine, or coffee depending on their taste for potables. Most of them took coffee. Hank asked twenty-four yen an hour for his work and most of them seemed relieved to find his demands reasonable.

In this manner the winter passed for Hank and Akiko. But despite the books and the repair work, the hunting hikes and the lovemaking, the seine hauling and the new friendships, Hank found himself with time not so much on his hands as on his mind.

"How did the words go," he wondered, "that song everybody sang one year in high school? *You on my hands and time on my mind and nothing but love in view.* That's sneaky, Mueller old son, and a little smart aleck, by Christ, to put that switcheroo in the first line. It's 'Time on my hands' and you know it. But it keeps coming up, doesn't it, pal? Because the lug that wrote the words to that song knew not how true he spoke. It's supposed to mean everything's wonderful when there's nothing but love in view. Hell, I'm the guy for whom it's true in the extreme sense of the word. That's all, brother. Look ahead as far as you can see and whadda you find? Nothing! Zero! Space! Vacuum! Time!

"Time above all, nothing but time, months and years and slow minutes of time, and you'll be twenty-eight years old the third of May, all dressed up in a blue kimono and no place to go. And nothing but love in view, don't forget. Does the time pass slowly, friend? Make a little love to fill the gaps. Do the years seem long, old deserter? How about a nice roll in the clover? Are you growing aweary like the Lady of Shalott? Try one of old Dr. Hank Mueller's beef injections. It'll do you a world of good, my friend.

"And are we all through with self-pity and remorse for

today, Mr. Mueller? Have you cried on your own shoulder because you're twenty-eight and not going anyplace? You did make your move with your round baby-blue eyes open, you know. No one put a pistol in your ribs to run a batch of currency through the old black market. She didn't wink at you the day you drove your jeep down that Shinjuku lane. Whose idea was the septic tank and the Stateside crapper and the gas heater? And who grabbed her by the little brown pinkie and towed her off to the boondocks to be your lover, nursemaid, and watchdog?

"All questions for sergeants, chum, and ones you can answer short and easy this time. But you ain't a sergeant any more and the big question's coming up: What the friggin' hell you gonna do about it?

"Why, that's just the right-size question, and one answer coming up: I'm gonna roll along with love on my hands and nothing, but nothing, in view until I get a gutful, and then I'll turn myself in and do my time . . ."

"I'll go back and stand trial and —"

"*Naniyo?*" asked Akiko fearfully across the table.

"What the hell, Baby-san! Was I thinkin' out loud again? Don't worry, old Hank's a little crazy."

"Never happen, crazy. You speak what you think. You say 'go back.'"

"I think we might go back to Tokyo sometime. Long time. Police forget."

And he held her close and lied on and on, until she looked up, smiling cheerily, pretending to believe him, and then turned her face away to shake her head and send the pair of tears flying from the corners of her cheekbones. For Akiko knew, had always known, had never doubted what they all knew, the Onlies and the whores and the virgins. "They always go back."

26

BUT he didn't go back that year or the next.
He only wanted to go in the bleak times when the monot-
ony of small-town life, the language barriers, the diet and
the dirt depressed him. But Hank was young and resilient.
At other times his Japanese neighbors and friends seemed
the best and the closest he had ever known, the country living healthy and the sea air a source of simple rapture. Mike
and the long country stalks after game were his safety
valve. They talked of everything, of books and authors, of
planes and pilots, of strategy and tactics, of morals and
customs, sex and marriage, and of war and peace.

Mike was a man of many parts, a thirty-four-year-old
bachelor, with a fine academic brain broadened by travel
and residence in the United States and tempered by war,
when he had flown a medium bomber. Hank liked to listen
to his Army experiences and countered with some of his
own. At times they would talk about Tarawa or Tinian,
with Mike describing the defeat from his bird's-eye view in
a battered Betty, and Hank filling in with his worm's-eye

view of the little battle sector where he crawled in the dust with an M-1 in one hand and a roll of telephone wire in the other.

One day they spoke cautiously of the war trials and ventured on the treacherous ground of atrocities. Hank began by feeling embarrassed for Mike and ended by feeling confused.

"Sure, it's rough in the line, I know, Mike," he said, "but you gotta admit the Japanese Army was loaded with sadistic bastards. I know the death march from Corregidor to Cabanatuan wasn't just propaganda. And that general of yours in Malaya got a pretty fair trial and admitted most of the charges, didn't he?"

"No question," Mike said. "They killed prisoners and they beat prisoners. But it wasn't sadism. It was a difference mainly of military attitudes. In our Army, beatings were common as discipline and not particularly important. Prisoners were sometimes killed because they couldn't be fed and transported and were too much nuisance. But I have heard that marines on Guadalcanal mowed down groups of Japanese who offered to surrender. They cut them off with machine guns when they came with hands in air. Perhaps that is only propaganda, too. You see, we lost the war, so we will never try anyone for war crimes."

"Well, about those prisoners on Guadalcanal. I heard the same thing. In fact, I know it's true, 'cause I know soldiers and marines who saw it happen. But always each act carries its own excuse. I don't know which comes first, the crime or the excuse, but the story I heard is that small groups of Japanese used the Americans' gullibility to fake surrenders. They would often come out with hands up in groups of three or four. One man would lead the others by a pace or two, and when they got within twenty-five yards, he'd trip and fall flat. On his back would be strapped one of your little twenty-seven-caliber machine guns, and one of the other soldiers would grab it and start spraying. Sometimes they'd wipe out a squad. Of course, it was a suicide act every time. They got wiped out in the end. The marines got suspicious of surrenders, especially if there was more than one in the group. They killed 'em, and sometimes, I suppose, they killed men who just plain wanted to surrender, no machine guns, no hand grenades in the armpit, nothing but wounds and sores and starvation they couldn't stand any more."

"I understand the action and the reason, Hank. However, to interpret this in the light of American or, more properly, Anglo-Saxon morality is difficult. When your men killed a prisoner, they were violating a major belief, a moral principle held in high regard by the Occident. When our men killed a prisoner, they paid him honor by using a military weapon, especially with a bayonet, and were being true to the *Bushido* code. Not always, of course. Many times they killed the helpless because they were trained to kill, and because of the inertia of killing which the heat of battle generates. And I think sometimes they killed for revenge because of hatred for Western superiority and fear of American and European colonialism. We Japanese are international claustrophobiacs. Our islands are too small, our land too poor, our reproduction rate too great. War was our safety valve. The pressure was inside."

"How about Hokkaido?" Hank asked. "You still haven't colonized your northern island completely. There's room for more people there."

"How about your Alaska? There's room for more people there also. We don't like snow and cold any better than Americans."

"Check. But you might do something about the population by birth control."

"What else? The government subsidizes contraception, teaches it to adults, makes devices available at cheap rates, prints pamphlets. We have even legalized abortions, and doctors and midwives are busy exterminating embryos. Last year in Omikura twenty-three women induced abortions with pointed sticks. Eleven of them died. But the population goes up — eighty-three million now, and one hundred million in ten years, they say."

"What do you think should be done?"

"I think we should walk carefully over this hill and see if the big *kiji* is sunning himself by the sugar-beet field."

They cradled their guns and moved slowly over the ridge.

And in the evenings, after they returned from the *ofuro*, their bodies lightly parboiled into a flamingo blush from the almost boiling water, Hank and Akiko would talk, shifting unpredictably from English to Japanese. For both of them it was easy to say in either language, "The sampan leaks badly again," or, "The price of eggs is always higher in the

[206]

winter." But an abstract concept was a difficult matter that had to be built up slowly, evolved with caution, many times requiring a pencil and paper sketch to support the idea, and sometimes abandoned without establishing a real exchange.

Inevitably they talked late into the night about their pasts. Akiko almost always responded to any expression of endearment or tenderness by adding another shocking chapter, as though to humble herself while she warned him how unworthy she was of his love.

"One thing I must speak, Ank-san. I was never marry. I just said damn big lie before." She held his big hand in her two while she confessed in a flat, expressionless voice. She seemed to invite his anger when she paused after such a statement, and she never defended herself or offered excuses.

"I bad girl long time. After high school I work for coal-business office in old Kaijo. One man he marry, my boss."

"A man married your boss?"

"Never happen. This boss man have wife, he my boss. He was very handsome and have *takusan* money."

"So you became his *koibito*?"

"*Hai.* Almost two year, but I never love him. I just catch *takusan* clothes that he give me, and he pay for apartment for me. My mother *takusan* worry. I make her big trouble and I make trouble for him, too. Then his wife think something. She make trouble —" Akiko held up two fingers — "double."

"I see. Trouble for both of you. So you got fired, I bet."

"Almost fire. Boss very kind. He make new job for me in Manchuria, so I have nice journey in big *junku*. First I go Sasebo and go on *junku*. Then we go to Korea to Jinsen, but I think Jinsen have new name, Intson."

"You mean Inchon?"

"*Hai*, Inchon. We stop two day and I go to big city, Korea number-one city, Keijo. But I think Keijo have new name, Sool."

"That's right. Seoul is the capital city. Inchon is the port."

"*Nan desuka*, 'port'?"

"Port, let me see. I mean the place where ships come all the time."

"So, so. Well, then, we go Antung, catch train, go Mukden, then go Changchun, then go small place name Kirin. Coal company have Manchuria office in this Kirin. But this office have other man, very high officer in coal company — boss officer. He like me because not many Japanese girl ever come to Kirin. He want to touch, so I catch *takusan* presents. Then I find one very handsome young man. He like me double and speak to marry me, but I bad girl and too much like rich man, so I want keep double." She held up the two telltale fingers.

"Uh-huh. You like keep rich man for presents and handsome man for love?"

"Not love. I told you, never love. I like handsome man for dance and sing and good time. I very dumb Japanese girl. Well, then, pretty soon more trouble. This young man get fire and go back Tokyo. Pretty soon I get fire and go

[208]

back Tokyo. That time we have war with United States and *takusan* officer and soldier spend money, so I no more working girls. I go teahouse and catch officer many times. Go many party, catch money. Then war finish. Period!"

She stabbed a forefinger in the air to indicate a period. She waited.

"I think you speak too much," he said and kissed her nose.

And on another night she ventured on the inevitable subject that consumes all wives and sweethearts on earth, his love life. After the tea and rice, the one evening cigarette, the question:

"How many woman *you* touch, Ank-san?"

For a moment he considered boosting the total and inventing a few torrid romances full of sex and fate and despair in the best Japanese tradition, but he decided against it. He was in this for the long pull and he couldn't be bothered to memorize his own lies.

"Not many," he said.

"Please, honey, tell me."

"I will tell you about the first time," he said, avoiding a direct answer. And he went on with the brief story, speaking sometimes in Japanese and sometimes in English.

"When I was not quite seventeen years old, I worked in summer for a garage, a civilian motor pool, you know, where people have cars washed and the motors repaired. Many high-school students in my country work in summer, when there is no school, to make money for clothes and good times. So one day I had to drive a car to a house a

[209]

short distance from this garage, because the woman who owned the car was calling on the telephone every few minutes and wanted the car in a big hurry. I came to the house and drove the car beside it and I went to the kitchen door and knocked. This was to give the woman the car keys. I had seen her once or twice when she brought the car to the station, the garage, you know, for gasoline. She was not young, maybe forty, maybe forty-five, and we had spoken a few times.

"She came to the door and asked me to come in. She had been drinking and she was stinko. I could smell the whiskey. And she was wearing a light kimono like the American women wear when they have just come from taking a bath. It was very hot weather at this time of year in Los Angeles. She wanted me to have a drink with her, so I said, 'Okay.' While she fixed the drinks she asked me all kinds of questions: How old was I. Did I like girls. Did I go on many petting parties.

"When she gave me the drink, the kimono was open and she wore nothing underneath. I was young and had never had a woman and I wanted her, although she was not pretty and smelled of whiskey and perfume. I never touched that drink and I only kissed her a little once and we went to bed. I was back at the garage in a half hour."

"You like?" she asked mischievously, smiling at him.

"Of course. Anyway, I think so. It happened so fast."

"That's because you young boy," said Akiko practically. "She have husband?"

"Yes, her husband worked in the city. Afterward she

came to the garage many times and wanted me to come see her when her husband was not at home. And she called on the telephone many, many times. I was afraid of trouble and went to another garage and got a new job. I did not see her again."

"I like story very much," said Akiko and clapped her hands in comic applause. "You tell me one story more, please."

So they told stories to each other. Hank told her about the great vineyards and the citrus groves of Southern California, the wide highways clotted with speeding automobiles, how wine was made from grapes, how a murder was committed in his neighborhood and the murderer apprehended later, how a boy friend of his got his girl pregnant and was forced to marry her. He translated with difficulty Ernest Hemingway's *Snows of Kilimanjaro* and Steinbeck's *Of Mice and Men*.

And Akiko in turn told how before the war the police were cruel and beat ignorant country people with their pistols if they failed to bow the prescribed number of times when asking simple directions, but now that the Americans were teaching "democracy," the police were better. She told the lovely legend of the faithful lover of the beautiful but heartless Omiya, who killed her at last in a suicide tryst in Atami, and how the willow which grew from the blood-stained earth even to this day droops its branches and sheds tears on the anniversary. And she told of bandit tribes in far mountain passes which had survived since ancient times and still robbed unwary travelers. She told of

[211   ]

the good times when there was plenty of food from the conquered areas of the empire and prices were low.

And of the days in Tokyo when the earth shook under the shadow of the B-29's, how every other house was razed to stop the raging fires, and how not one brick remained on another between the RTO station and the Imperial Moat. And about the lovely girl dramatic troupe, the Takarazuka review, and how the kabuki theater movement was established.

So the months passed.

27

By SPRING of 1950 the wild inflation spiral of the yen hit three hundred sixty to one dollar. In April Hank and Akiko were still living in Omikura, but the hoard they had brought with them from Tokyo had disappeared during the winter. The original amount had dwindled to one twentieth of its value, due to the devaluation of the yen. As their reserve vanished, they cut down more and more on their Occidental tastes for expensive items, until they no longer bought cigarettes, sugar, candy, or clothing from the Ona black market. Their food was the same as that of all the people of Omikura; their house was, if anything, more barely furnished than most. Hank had one pair of much-cobbled low shoes but wore wooden geta and the coarse coverall ordinarily.

However, Hank was able to keep the food and rent budget current with his earnings from fishing and mechanical repair jobs. Some months his income was as much as fifteen thousand yen, and once when they hit a fine school of king mackerel, their seining brought a catch which they sold for thirty thousand yen. As a result he could figure on an income equivalent to thirty or forty dollars a month. Three times while they lived in Omikura Akiko made trips into Tokyo and returned with clothing and extra money. The money, she said, was from rent on her two houses, part of which her mother had saved for her. Four times Hank wrote a note to Bill Zarnowski, which was passed to Sumiko in Ona and relayed to Bill through Yōko. Bill complied with the requests faithfully, sending Sumiko back to Ona with generous supplies of shotgun shells, cartons of cigarettes, soap, razor blades, socks, and two first-aid kits.

They only smoked a rare cigarette of the inferior Japanese tobacco and Akiko immediately converted the cigarettes from Bill into more yen on the Ona black market. She bought a large tin bathtub and insisted on giving Hank and herself their baths instead of paying the small fee at the public *ofuro*. They rarely cooked fish or sea food, eating it raw after leaving it twenty-four hours in heavy brine, and flavoring it with a dip of spiced oil. Game and chance bits of meat were sliced into thin strips so they would cook quickly without wasting charcoal. Hank and Akiko were lean and healthy and always a little hungry.

"You are one of the privileged few, old son," Hank told himself more than once. "Only you out of all the millions of servicemen know exactly how it feels to be a Jap. Maybe you and a few prisoners and a few other guys that went into the bush for a year or so. You dine on boiled rice and raw fish and dream of malted milks. The thought of a stick of gum fills your mouth with saliva. You live in a clean

[214   ]

house and bathe every day, but in the morning you pick your way carefully down the cobbled street between rivulets of fresh urine where every man and child relieves himself in front of his house. You sniff the fresh salt of the sea wind and gag at the reek of rotting fish. You walk in the green fertile countryside and admire the yellowing grain, but the very earth of paddy fields smells of excrement.

"Yes, sir, kid, you've gone Asiatic and then some. To be a Jap is to live better than you believed possible two years ago on forty bucks a month (sometimes only twenty-five). And it's to live worse, unable to reach in your pocket for a cigarette or the price of a beer, to sleep on the floor without fresh sheets on washday, and to be a little hungry all the time."

28

HE AWOKE quickly and silently sometime in
the night with the rip of heavy rain on the tiles overhead
and Akiko's body slim and straight in sleep beside him on
the pallet, and for the first few seconds he listened for danger in the noises of the night and the rain. It was the old
feeling of waking in a foxhole at night with danger thick in
the air and the room, and the silence. But almost with relief he found himself awakened by a sensation stranger to
him than the danger of human-wave attacks or the stealthy
infiltration of enemy patrols, stranger but still familiar
enough to be identified. He was sick.

So he lay, supine, and felt the nausea come in waves that
seemed to rise in his guts and roll toward his throat, but
each time he fought down the wave before it broke. Each
time the waves got stronger and he knew it would be the
next one or the next, so between waves he rose and
switched on the light and got a pail from the kitchen and
put a little water in the bottom. He put the pail on the
tatami beside the pallet and lay down again as another

wave rolled through the secret canals of his body, and Akiko awoke.

She sat up quickly and faced him, with the little head shake with which she always dismissed sleep and a tiny smile as of one who expects to be pleasantly surprised by the novelty of awakening at an unusual hour, and inquired, "What is it?"

"Sick," he said briefly, unable to trust his voice, for the waves were stronger and closer together now.

She saw the pail, and his skin the color of bleached sand, and the sweat running from his forehead. Just then he rose to his knees and was convulsed, his head bent over the pail, which he grasped with both hands on the rim, and it was a sickness like none he had known, with a pain deep inside like the stirring of a gut wound after the first sucrete of morphine begins to wear off. And he knew that the feeling when he had first wakened in the dark, born of foxholes and fear, had been true — that there was danger in this sickness. But immediately he felt relieved, almost buoyant by contrast with his retching misery of a moment past, and reached for a cigarette.

"Ank-san, what makes you sick? You never catch sick before."

"Gunso and I split a beer at the hotel after work tonight. Musta got hold of a green bottle. I'll be all right now."

"You drink *takusan?*"

"No, just the one bottle. We each drank half. Sometimes you get a green bottle. It was that damn Chiba beer I never liked."

"You eat something with Gunso? Maybe hotel food no good."

"Yeah, I ate some oysters fried *tempura* style. Maybe it was the oysters."

But the waves came rolling back, bigger waves and rushing faster out of control, and he hung over the bucket a long time, while she held his head and laid him gently back on the *tatami* to mop his face with a wet cloth. And now he felt the pain all the time, even between the spasms of nausea deep inside, and he knew it was bad.

"I'll be all right for a while now, hon. Run down and wake up Mike and ask him to come. If this goes on, I'll need a man to help. Don't worry. I can help myself."

She whimpered a little at leaving, looked helplessly about the room, and then slipped into a kimono and pair of wooden geta, emptied the foul bucket of vomit into the rain-washed street, put fresh water in the pail by his bed, and clattered away over the cobbles. The receding staccato of wooden clogs on the cobbled street was to him the essence of danger in a Japanese city at night. It was the drumbeat of haste and violence, heard often in the deep of night, the sound that marked the urgency of flight, or the relentlessness of pursuit.

But he had little time to think now, for he was vomiting almost continuously while she was gone, empty now, and retching in painful, quick, straining spasms into the pail. The vomit was uniformly viscous and brown and appeared to be composed of solids that resembled fine coffee grounds, and at the end of each spasm there were little ropes of red. The taste in his mouth was like dirty copper filings.

Alone now, he knew fear, for he was a stranger to this sort of sickness. He had been seasick most of one day on a transport out of San Francisco during the war, and once in high school he had gotten briefly and violently sick on wine. And he had been wounded and learned a little how to handle pain, but this was different. It was deeper and bigger, and he missed the vast sense of the Army's powerful impersonal organization behind him, the white-coated doctors and corpsmen, the long antiseptic corridors of ready beds, the cabinets of medicines and drugs, and the clipped, efficient American voices.

But the door panel slid back even as his anxiety mounted and Akiko and Mike came in, quickly kicking off their clogs below the gallery, and Mike knelt by the pallet and looked at him for a time. Then he looked in the pail.

"How do you feel now, Hank?" he asked.

"Not so good. Must be something I ate or drank. Is there a doctor nearer than Ona, Mike?"

"No doctor. I woke up Gunso and Dr. Miyaguchi. They will be here soon."

"Christ, a veterinarian."

"A man is not so different from an ox when he is sick. He will know what to do."

And after that he remembered only little bits, when he rallied after a particularly violent and protracted convulsion. He heard Gunso and Mike and Akiko talking in whispers about moving him, saying that there would be no

[219]

bus for Ona before ten o'clock and the roads were in such a state with the heavy June rains they were reluctant to try it in a motorcycle cab. He remembered the veterinarian, Miyaguchi-san, who came close behind Gunso and looked in the pail before he looked at anything else and spoke quickly to Mike. And even smaller things he sensed — more people coming, the rhythm of the litter as he was carried downhill, the spatter of rain on his face, and the smell of the harbor.

And the quick, low words that came through his web of pain, getting dimmer now, because Miyaguchi-san had given him something that was helping him black out.

"He is bleeding inside. The old blood is brown, but there is not much new blood. Miyaguchi-san says he will be all right if we get him to the hospital." That was Mike.

"In the boat he can rest. We will be in Chiba in two hours." Gunso was speaking reassuringly to Akiko, who cried quietly, holding the pail ready beside his head as he was carried along.

And he felt the familiar thrust and roll of the wooden deck under his back and the strong voice of the engine. Once, for a little time, he felt the heavy hands of the sea twisting at the hull around him and knew they were outside the harbor. And he felt the touch of tiny rain-wet hands that snugged the blankets about him and mopped his face with cloths wrung out in cool sea water. Then for a space he knew nothing.

He was conscious next of the lights of a strange room and

the man he knew was a doctor, the way you always know a doctor, and the argument going on in Japanese.

"Yes, an operation, and quickly. But I cannot touch an American. I am sorry, but I must report this. No, at once. I will give medicine, now."

And he heard Akiko's voice begging the doctor not to report, and the wildness and hysteria that must have gone on for a long time, and he felt ashamed for her, because she begged so vainly, and for himself, because he wanted the doctor to send for the Army. He roused himself then, and knew he was weak, but he had not vomited for quite a while, and his voice was steady.

"It is no use, Akiko. I must call the Army. Ask the doctor to show us the telephone."

And Akiko suddenly was restored by the decision, as long as Hank had made it, glad even that he had decided to end it, and that he would live by his decision, live, even in a cell in America, just so that somewhere on the weary face of the planet he would be alive and would be Hank.

They wheeled him to a telephone in a sort of office, wheeled him on a high table, and placed the call to PMO at GHQ and handed him the phone.

"My name is Sergeant Henry Mueller, 91st Engineers. I am in Yodobashi Hospital in Chiba and very sick. Please send an ambulance."

They wheeled him, still on the table, through almost dark corridors, and he was sick and blacked out again, but remembered sometime (it must have been in the Chiba hospital) the needle in his elbow vein, held by a strip of tape, and the big bottle of clear liquid that hung above and beside him. The waterlike liquid bubbled quietly, and when the bubbles subsided, the level of the liquid was a bit lower in the inverted bottle, and after a while he knew they were draining the bottle into his veins. When next he remembered the bottle, it was being held aloft by a corpsman in a careening ambulance, and another corpsman was holding him strongly on the curves of the wet streets, and feeling the arms bracing him and seeing and smelling the khaki uniforms, he was no longer afraid. For he was back in the hands of the Army, the good old Army of the United States, the Army of hatreds and miracles, the men in OD cloth who could scatter a handful of lives with a spoken word as a pinch of seasoning in the putrid brew of war, but the same khaki empire that protected, that sewed the shrapnel-ripped viscera with casual precision, that restored the spilled blood in the flaccid vessels, that cleverly molded the mascerated flesh, and delicately wired the splintered bones. He was safe. He slept.

29

Finally it was over, the vomiting, the diarrhea, and the pain. He was alone in a four-bed ward, remembering in flashes the many bottles of saline solution and whole blood that had been emptied into his veins, the chalky-tasting jelly he had swallowed that soothed the spasm-knotted entrails, the brisk, earthy humor of the nurses as they slid the bedpans under or out and bore them away with queenly carriage.

He tried to think and to plan, but it was too much effort, and he watched the window, in great weariness and relief, for the brief arc of a bird's flight or the arrowy passage of an aircraft, sleeping, waking, and sleeping again. Days went on and on through electrocardiograms, X rays, and stool specimens. He was on bathroom privileges on the ninth day, could walk to the elevator, ride to the main floor, and shop in the hospital PX.

The doctor paid him a brief call on the tenth day.

"Acute gastroenteritis is what we call it. Severe food poisoning might be simpler. We have examined you carefully and can't find any ulcer or focus for your gastric hemorrhage. Apparently the infection in your intestinal tract was so severe that a lot of capillaries ruptured. You had what might be called a close one. You were fibrillating badly when they brought you in and we thought you had a permanent heart condition at first, but your cardiograms are rapidly returning to normal. We'll keep you here another week or ten days to clear up the parasites in your intestinal tract. Man, you sure were wormy."

He hesitated, rubbed his sandpapery jowl, took another look at Hank's chart, and spoke in a slightly embarrassed manner.

"Just call it an acute illness. No reason to expect a recurrence, and no permanent damage. I'm supposed to tell you you're restricted to the hospital. We had quite a time identifying you from your dog tags. Couldn't find anyone who'd ever heard of you until we located Captain Zarnowski. He'll be up to see you soon, I expect. I'm letting you have visitors starting today."

Bill came that same afternoon. He had captain's bars on his collar but was otherwise unchanged.

"Hello, Bill."

"Hello, Hank."

"See you made captain."

"The Army's hard up. How's the old Geronimo, son? Feelin' any pain?"

"Comin' back fast. I'll be ready to play grab-ass with these nurses pretty soon. Have you heard from Akiko?"

"Saw her twice. She doesn't say much but said to tell you

they weren't bothering her. She's living at home. I brought a package of your clothes she gave me, and she said to remind you there was a hundred-dollar bill in your leather belt."

"How's Yōko?"

"We broke it off six months ago. She wanted me to install a revolving door on her bedroom, so she could handle two-way traffic during my working hours. I got tired of waiting in line."

"Tough when they bounce like that. She was sure beautiful."

"Too beautiful. She found out how much her beauty was worth. The little bitch was born with a cash register for a heart. Never mind the horns on your Polack, skivvy boy. Tell me what you need and what I can do."

Hank thought for a minute. There was some appeal behind Zarnowski's words. It was what he could do for Zarnowski. For he was beyond anybody's help and the knowledge filled him with simple compassion. All he could do now was be a good joe.

"Before I took the powder, when they were questioning me at C.I.D., I found out they were looking for a wad of greenbacks that I couldn't account for. I still can't, and I won't guess. Akiko doesn't know anything about it either. That's where it'll stay. No, don't tell me anything, Bill. Just leave it lay. I like it better that way."

Bill's dark face was red and he twisted his cap in his long fingers.

"That damn bitch, Yōko. She must be a low-grade millionaire now by Japanese standards. Don't foul yourself up by trying to cover —"

"Skip it, Bill. I'll tell them what I know, and that's all. No one's involved except me and they know all about that, anyway."

After that they were both embarrassed and uneasy. They talked briefly and with manifest constraint and shook hands with relief.

"Keep a tight asshole, son. They can't hang you."

"I will. So long, Bill."

"If there's anything I can do —"

"I'll let you know."

"I'll keep in touch with you."

"Good-by now."

"Good-by."

It was no good, because they had nothing to say to each other, not even good-by, no spoken word that didn't betray hypocrisy and self-interest, no common emotion except a thin thread of fear. By contrast, Hank received First Lieutenant George Yamamoto with a feeling of unrealistic welcome. At least they had something to talk about and Yamamoto was the best talker of the C.I.D. officers who had interviewed him two years ago. Besides, he wanted to get it over with, fast.

"How are we going to go about this?" Yamamoto asked when he came to see him. "You are something of an embarrassment, Mueller. Lieutenant Taliaferro and Captain Wentland aren't here any more, so you're my problem. Are you still as difficult a problem as I remember you?"

"Not nearly. I softened up out in the boondocks. Tell me, how can I save you labor, Lieutenant?"

"Just tell me the story."

"You know the story. I got a friend in L.A. to draw my savings from the bank and ship them to me, three thousand dollars in blue-seal currency. I ran it through the black-market Chinaman in Shinjuku, a hundred and two hundred dollars' worth at a time. I converted some of the yen and stashed over half of it away. What I converted into scrip I sent back to the bank in small amounts in money orders. The rest I lived up in Tokyo and out in the back country when I was hid out. You know how the yen has been devalued. That wiped out most of my roll in the last two years."

"You had a particular reason for wanting to make money fast?"

"Not a good one. Just hungry for a fast buck, because it seemed easy and I wanted a good time for free."

"Where did you hide the money you kept?"

"Different places. Mostly in the cushions of my jeep, in the padding. Later I stuffed it in the barrels of my double-barreled shotgun. That's where it was when I ran off."

"I see. Now, you were brought here from Yodobashi Hospital in Chiba by some fishermen from Omikura. I suppose that's where you had been living."

"Look here, Lieutenant, you won't bother those people in Omikura? They had nothing to do with it. I told everyone I was discharged."

"I don't see any reason to involve them, Sergeant.

That's not our business, and we won't ask the Japanese police to investigate without reason. One other question I can't figure out from your story: Why did you run away from the charges in the first place? The prospect of living with these Japanese must not have been *that* attractive, and I can hardly believe you meant to make a lifetime career of hiding in a native fishing village."

"Well, Lieutenant, the real reason was I found out you were grilling my girl friend and that the Japanese police were abusing her. I figured I could take the heat off her, because she didn't have anything to do with it, and I didn't want her persecuted any more."

"She assist you in escaping?"

"No, I dragged her along against her will, talked her into it. I kept her with me by threats. I told her I'd have her sent away to an American prison if she left and turned me in. I said —"

Yamamoto held up his hand with a wide grin.

"Easy, Mueller. You don't have to make it that strong. I'm trying to sort out enough to make up a confession for you to sign. One that will hold water. Don't make like Eugene O'Neill before a general court."

Yamamoto thought for a moment, smoking and looking out the window, teetering back against the wall in the straight-backed chair by the bed. He spoke quietly, still staring out the window.

"You love this girl?"

"Yes."

"What do you want to do about it?"

"Serve my time, and come back and marry her."

Yamamoto shook his head and looked at Hank straight then.

"Marriage is out, Mueller. You can't have a damn thing on your record under GHQ regulations if you want to marry a Japanese girl. That lets you out. She has to be investigated politically, morally, socially, and every which way. That lets her out."

"This occupation will end before I'm through with this business. There'll be a peace treaty, and it'll just be between ourselves."

George Yamamoto nodded thoughtfully. "That's always a possibility," he said.

Then he faced Hank and stubbed out his cigarette on the bedside stand.

"Look here, Mueller. I want this case tied up as quickly as possible. From what you tell me I can see you do, too. It's apparent you want to protect your Japanese friends and the woman, Akiko Watanabe. I think I can help you do that. There is a charge against Akiko by the Japanese police, but I can fix it so she'll get off with a fine. She's not broke. She owns two good houses and has a couple of fat savings accounts in Tokyo banks, so she'll get off easy. I'll follow the case and see she isn't mistreated.

"I'm going to bring you a confession that covers your violation of the currency regulations and the desertion to avoid prosecution. I'll fix it to cover some of the obvious gaps in your story. That's all I can do for you. If you plead guilty and cite your excellent record as a soldier, I think you'll get a reasonably short sentence. Is that what you want?"

"That's what I want."

"We'll leave you here until the doctor says you're ready for transfer to the detention barracks. Is there anything I can do for you?"

"Can I see Akiko?"

Yamamoto thought that one over briefly.

"Once. Here in the hospital. Later perhaps we can arrange for her to be admitted for a visit before you're shipped out. I think you'll like it better here in the hospital. I'll get word to her. I know where she is."

He rose and picked up his briefcase.

"I'll be back when I get the papers ready for you to sign. Couple of days, I expect."

"I'll wait right here," Hank said.

He waked at the sound of her voice murmuring a soft "Thank you" in the familiar, lilting, little-girl voice, and rolling his head drowsily, saw her completing a formal bow to the nurse who had showed her to the room. He smiled but didn't say anything as she came toward him and she smiled brightly and quickly in answer. The nurse followed her in, lowered the window an unnecessary notch, and left quickly, pulling the door almost shut as she left.

"How you, Ank-san?"

"Fine, Baby. Army doctors fixed me up O.K."

"You too much thin, I think. You have plenty food?"

"Sure thing. Lots of food."

"Well, then." She seated herself on the bedside chair and

smiled again determinedly. They were silent, wondering how to begin, and what there was to say, and Hank, at least, wondered if it was worth while saying anything. But Akiko plunged, as she always did, straight into the very crux, bypassing all commonplaces almost contemptuously.

"What you think Army do now — to you, I mean?"

She was pronouncing her words carefully, sounding most of her *th*'s as he had tried to teach her.

"I think I will have a general court-martial soon. Then I must go back to America to an army prison. Maybe lucky — only four, five years. Lieutenant Yamamoto is making everything easy."

"I know." She nodded vigorously, her heavy page-boy hair swinging energetically past her cheeks. "Lieutenant Yamamoto is very kind. To me. I think Japanese-police trouble soon finish. I must pay *takusan* money, but no more punch."

She made a small hooked punch toward her own chin in comic imitation of one of Hank's favorite gestures. They both laughed.

"When I finish prison, I think Japan and United States will have peace. Then I will come back to Japan and we can marry."

Her bright little face clouded swiftly and she sat scowling at her shoes like a sullen child.

"I don't think so."

"Why not?"

"No damn good. I would not make good wife for you. Japan is not good country for you. I long time bad girls before. Best for you, Ank-san, you forget, and catch nice Stateside girls for marry. One thing I wish —"

"What is it you wish?"

"I wish I have baby. I wish catch boy-san. Pretty soon old and nobody come my house. I like nice little boy. Then when I old woman have big strong boy-san and he be very kind to me."

"When I come back, we'll have two, three baby-san, honey."

"Never happen baby-san. Please, Ank-san, no speak about come back. I want you forget Akiko. Maybe I forget, too, sometime. I think I can do."

He watched her face and saw the trembling lips and the tense little fists in her lap as she lied valiantly, trying in a desperate moment to renounce their four years, in order to make it easier for him.

"I love you, Akiko," he said.

She smiled and the tears slid quickly down onto her cheekbones and she flicked them away with an impatient shake of her head as she opened the calfskin bag and rummaged for something among the contents. She came up with a snapshot enlargement he had given her in 1948 that showed him at the wheel of his jeep, grinning cockily into the lens.

"Please," she choked, crying harder now. "You sign."

He took the cheap ball-point pen and wrote quickly across the foreground of the photograph. *All my love — until I come back to you, Hank.*

He handed it to her and said the words out loud. She

leaned toward him and held out her arms and looked questioningly toward the door.

"Can I?"

"Why not?"

He got to his feet and kissed her, holding her lightly and easily, feeling his heart start to race and skip, so that he swayed a little and felt her arms tighten and her tiny body brace him with unbelievable strength.

They parted reluctantly as though drawn by a vast invisible force, clasped arms sliding across bodies and shoulders and curled fingers sliding down the warm arms until the hands said good-by to the hands and the finger tips fell away into the unfeeling air.

"Tell me what to do." They were at the door now.

"Wait," he said. "Wait for me."

And she was gone down the corridor with a light clatter of spike heels on the gleaming tiles.